CLINGING TO RAINBOWS

CLINGING TO RAINBOWS

Aussie Sky Series

Jenny Glazebrook

To Rob

You understand me like no other human does.
Life is a joy with you by my side and I thank God for you.
Thank you for always looking at my first drafts,
and for all your valuable suggestions.
I love your humour and your written edits often make me laugh.
Your encouragement and support are invaluable.
I love you more than I ever dreamed possible.

Chapter One

Storm Clements glared into the sunset. Another day done. His boss was pleased, but that didn't bring any satisfaction. How long would he be stuck working on the roads?

The shrill ring of the phone in his pocket jarred him. He wiped strong, dirt-worn hands down his work pants before reaching for it. The screen flashed one name—Prince. His brother. He jabbed his finger onto the pick-up symbol. Better take it.

'What?' He didn't care that he growled the words. He was in a bad mood.

'Storm, there's been a bit of an emergency. They put Rachel in for observation. Her blood pressure is way too high and it's risky for her and the twins. They might have to deliver them early.'

Storm felt his heart miss a beat. 'Okay.'

What else was he supposed to say? His siblings would have promised to pray but he wasn't going to pretend. He wasn't a praying man. Drama made him uncomfortable.

'Keep me updated?' There, that sounded like he wasn't heartless, but didn't sound soppy, either.

'I will. Just wanted to let you know.'

There was pain in Prince's voice and Storm shook his head. If you were silly enough to let yourself love, you were going to get hurt. It was as simple as that.

'Bye.' He knew he sounded short but Prince should be used

to that. He shoved his phone back in his pocket and moved toward the horse grazing in the grass a few metres away.

'Dusty Lane.'

The animal lifted its head and Storm put his arms around his neck. As he did, his mind filled with memories of Prince's wife, Rachel. Storm didn't like many people in the world, but he had to admit he liked Rachel. He didn't like the idea of the world without her in it.

She was the girl who had stepped into the path of a punch meant for him during a high school fight in his early teen years. He'd been disgusted at the time; a girl coming to his rescue. But she'd taken the broken nose meant for him. She appeared all sweet and gentle but she was tough.

In one smooth bound he leaped onto his horse's back. 'Come on, Dusty. We'd better head to the hospital.'

***

Tori Seeth shivered and folded her slender arms across her chest. Light shone through the window and onto the street, warmth in its glow. Yet she felt a chill every time she walked into that house. It wasn't home. But then, where was home?

She had to go in. There was nowhere else. Besides, if she didn't go back, what would become of Sarah? Taking a deep breath, she opened the door.

'And where do you think you've been?'

Her mother stepped out from behind the door and stood centimetres from her face, breathing a hot challenge on her forehead. Tori dared not cringe when she smelt the alcohol on her mother's breath. Fear gave Mum power; a power she couldn't afford to let her have. She stared back. 'I needed some air.'

A leering smile crossed her mother's face. Trouble was coming. 'Air? I'll make you need some air.'

Cold, vice-like hands came around her neck. She didn't

move a muscle, but looked steadily into her mother's eyes. They narrowed a moment before she stepped back. 'You're lucky we've got an audition coming up.'

Another modelling audition. She had to look perfect. Her mother would never risk leaving marks around her neck.

Where was Sarah? She darted a glance around the room.

'What, don't you trust me?'

Tori recognised the threat in her mother's tone. Sarah wasn't safe here. If a woman could treat her own daughter the way Tori was treated, how could she expect her to treat Sarah any better?

She took a risk. 'Mum, what about when her father comes back to get her?'

'Ha! He won't come back. Didn't you hear him? He hates me.'

'But Mick doesn't hate Sarah. How could he? He's her father.' She forced herself not to flinch as her mother shoved her against the wall.

'How dare you! I told you never to mention the name of that little witch's father again!' The outstretched hand came down across her face with a resounding slap.

Tori forced herself to keep her hands at her side. Reaching to the place on her stinging cheek would let her mother know she had hurt her. 'But Mum, you've never stayed in a relationship that long before. I thought you must care for each other at least a little bit.' Tori wondered at her own courage. Every word fuelled Mum's temper and the angrier she became, the more irrational she was. It was dangerous, but for Sarah, she would play with fire.

Her mother let out a howl that sounded like a wild animal. She poked a shaking finger at her nose. Her face was bright red and beads of sweat were forming on her forehead. 'You have no idea about anything! Your own father left as soon as he knew I was expecting you. I should have listened to him. I should have aborted you when I had the chance. Don't know what I was thinking.'

Tori knew what she had been thinking. Her mother had

screamed it into her face before. She wanted the welfare payments. Then once Tori had been born beautiful she used her to make money from modelling and beauty pageants.

She wasn't allowed to mention her father, but often she wondered about him. Why was he so determined not to have a child? Had he known how her mother would treat her?

A sound caught her attention. Dishes clattering in the sink. Sarah was washing up. She shouldn't be doing that. The infection in her foot was so bad she could hardly stand. But at least she was alive. Tori felt the bulge of the medicine in her back pocket and sent up a prayer that it wouldn't be found.

A groan sounded as Sarah moved and Tori made herself bide her time. Once the lights were off and her mother was in bed she would help her.

It was almost midnight when the house was finally quiet, except for Sarah's tossing and turning. Tori crept down the hallway, pausing after each step, avoiding the floorboards that always creaked.

'Tori?' Sarah sat up in bed. Her fair hair hung limp around her shoulders and some stuck to her damp forehead.

'I brought you some medicine.'

Sarah's eyes widened in the dim light. 'Where'd you get that?'

'Patrick. His grandfather always gets infections. It's from his last repeat of antibiotics he didn't get filled. Patrick reckons it has to be better than nothing.'

Their whispered voices sounded loud in the silence of the night, but Tori knew her mother slept deeply once she had relaxed herself with enough alcohol. *If* she was asleep. She had to be. Their safety depended on it.

Tori handed Sarah a bottle of water and a tablet from the foil pack. 'Three a day, it says.'

Sarah nodded and put a tablet in her mouth before taking a gulp of water. Her breathing was rapid. The tablets needed to work. Fast. The infection was getting worse.

Sarah wiped at her fevered brow. 'Tori, I don't think Dad's coming back.'

Tori didn't answer but her mind replayed the scene of a week ago, the last time they had seen Sarah's father. Her mother screamed and cursed, accusing him of stealing money. Sarah's father had yelled back. Plates were thrown across the kitchen and Sarah's father ended up with a cut over one eye. Sarah tried to intervene and ended up with a cut on her foot from the broken crockery. It wasn't anything unusual. He always came back a few days later, but that time he hadn't.

'Tori?'

Tori forced herself to look at Sarah. She couldn't deny it. Her mother wouldn't be treating Sarah this way if she thought he was coming back.

'Your father said he wants nothing to do with you,' her mother had spat into Sarah's face that morning. 'You're a loser, just like him.'

'What are we going to do?' Sarah's trembling question brought Tori back to the present.

'First we're going to get you better. Then we're getting out of here. You and me. We're old enough to find work. We'll find a place of our own.'

Sarah's eyes widened. 'She'll find us.'

It was a possibility, but Tori was determined to take them as far from her mother and the abuse as she could. They would run. They would find work. They would go to a women's refuge if they had to. Whatever it took. And they would have each other.

'She's scared, you know. That's why she's being so awful, Sarah. She's scared that together we're stronger than her. She's scared she's losing control of us. And she is.'

For the first time, Sarah smiled and a light came to her eyes. Tori recognised it as hope. Hope was something she had not allowed herself to feel for a long time. She almost smiled back.

'If we play this right, we could be out of here in a week. So you make sure you get enough rest and take those tablets.'

Sarah nodded and hid the box of antibiotics under her pillow. Their lives and freedom depended on them.

Tori went to stand, but Sarah reached for her hand. 'Why does she hate me so much?'

The pain in the broken whisper tore at Tori's heart. She tried so hard to protect Sarah but she'd failed. She took Sarah's hand and worried about how warm and clammy it was. 'It's not you she hates. It's your strength.'

'Huh?'

Tori leaned closer. 'You have to believe me, Sarah. Don't let her destroy who you are. You're strong. You're talented, clever, everything she isn't.'

Sarah let out a mirthless laugh. 'I wish. But I think it's because I'm not any of those things. And I'm not beautiful like you. You have all those modelling trophies, you won all those beauty pageants ...'

Tori cut her off with a shake of her head. 'She doesn't love me, either.' The truth hurt but she had to tell it. No more hiding it from the girl to protect her. 'If I don't win, she hates me.'

Sarah leaned forward. 'But you always win.'

'Not always.'

Sarah's eyes turned dark. 'And if you don't win, what happens?'

Tori bit her lip, then slowly lifted her shirt. 'There's a reason I never do bikini modelling.'

Sarah let out a gasp and Tori closed her eyes for a brief moment. The hidden bruises were a constant reminder of what would happen if she failed. And in her mother's eyes, not winning was failing.

She remembered back to the times she'd displeased her mother. She remembered her mother's outstretched hand, raised to slap her when she wasn't dressed quickly enough and was disqualified from the judging. She remembered the time a dark-skinned girl had won. She had never seen such a sweet face. The girl had large, beautiful eyes and dark hair with ringlets curling about her face and a shine in her eyes that Tori knew she had never had. Those eyes had shone of hope and joy; something Tori had never experienced. But her mother couldn't see that, and had grabbed her own daughter by the hand and dragged her to the car.

'Why didn't you smile, Victoria?' She pounded her fists into Tori's rib cage, over and over.

'I did,' Tori cried, but her mother was infuriated by the defence and gave one final blow to Tori's head which left her lying dizzy and still, unable to breathe normally. By the time they arrived home, her mother seemed to have calmed down, but Tori couldn't forget the awful ache in her heart which went much deeper than her throbbing head and the pain in her chest. For as long as she could remember she had been used to earn money and satisfy her mother's infatuation with beauty.

Throughout the night, Tori listened to Sarah's unsteady breathing and suppressed moans. Why bother pretending she could sleep? She knew it was impossible. Light finally crept under the bedroom blinds. Morning always promised hope of a new beginning and a better day. If only that promise could be realised today. It *had* to be. Throwing a dressing gown around her shoulders, she made her way to Sarah's room. The girl looked surreal, her eyelashes appearing too dark against her pale cheeks. For one horrible moment she wondered if she was even alive. She reached out a trembling hand. Her forehead was warm—too warm.

'Sarah, can I get you some water?' There was no response. She tried again. 'Please wake up.'

Her eyes fluttered open and she looked dazedly at Tori and spoke with effort through parched lips. 'Don't cry, Tori.'

Tori hadn't felt the drops rolling down her cheeks until that moment. She wiped them away. 'You need a doctor.'

Sarah's mouth turned up in one corner but it was clear it was an effort. 'It's okay. I've got you, haven't I?'

Tori nodded through her tears. 'Yes, you'll always have me.' Warmth crept around her heart. No one had loved her until Sarah had come to live with them.

She studied Sarah's blonde hair that needed a wash so badly and the dark shadows under her eyes. She knew it was in stark contrast with her own carefully styled long curls and clear, moisturised skin. Lash extensions would be added before the audition tomorrow and her mother would make her put in her blue tinted contact lenses and apply make-up. She wouldn't be allowed to eat today. Her stomach needed to be tight and toned.

How could two completely different methods of abuse have the same effect? She and Sarah both lived in fear, under her mother's control.

'Here, have another tablet.' Tori reached under the pillow and took out the packet. Carefully, she undid the foil, all the while listening for the creak of a floorboard that would indicate her mother was awake.

She sighed in relief as Sarah swallowed it. But then she suddenly lurched forward, choking on the water. Panic filled her eyes as she coughed and spluttered. Tori didn't know what to do first, hide the tablets or help Sarah. She couldn't hear anything but Sarah's coughs, and her mother was sure to have heard them too. She saw Sarah's eyes widen and followed her gaze to the door, while attempting to tuck the box of tablets under the sheets.

Her mother stood there, eyes cold and calculating, pinning her to the spot. 'I told you not to come in here.'

Anger rose up inside Tori. 'Sarah's sick. She needed me.'

Her mother took a step forward and Tori felt the light pressure of Sarah's fingers on hers. A glance at Sarah's pleading eyes quieted her.

'Sick?' Her mother stepped forward, whipped back the sheet

and looked at the box of tablets. With a snort, she tossed them onto the floor, then ground them into the floor with her foot. 'Sarah's not sick. She's lazy. A whining loser like her father. Now go and get ready for school.'

Tori fought an inner battle. If she stood up to her mother, both she and Sarah would be in danger. But if she went to school, Sarah would be alone with her mother.

'Go, Tori. I'll see you this afternoon.' Sarah's words were quiet, her look pleading. Slowly, Tori stood. Sarah gave her a brave look as she left the room. She didn't find it convincing.

It was impossible to concentrate in class. Maths was usually her favourite subject. Numbers and formulas were safe and consistent in her unpredictable world, but that day flashes of Sarah's last brave expression played in her mind. Surely there was something she could do?

'Are you okay?'

She looked up to where Patrick stood before her. Patrick, the boy with honest, alive eyes. Even the gold-rimmed glasses they hid behind did little to take away from their expression.

'I'm okay.' She tried busying herself with setting up her text book.

'You sure?'

She shrugged, knowing he was genuinely concerned. Many people asked her the same question, but it was different when Patrick asked. 'It's Sarah. She's still sick.'

'Sick or hurt?'

Tori swallowed. How should she answer that? She had seen the way Patrick's discerning eyes often focussed on Sarah's bruises. She always explained them away in a cheerful, easy-going way that left no room for more questions or suspicion. But she knew Patrick wasn't fooled.

'Did you give her the antibiotics?'

Tori nodded.

'She'll be okay then.' He almost smiled, and she only wished it were true. She couldn't tell Patrick what Mum had done. He would be like every other person trying to help; he would put himself in danger or make it worse for both her and Sarah.

Patrick was studying her with probing eyes as though trying to work out what she wasn't saying. 'Are you missing her?'

'She gives me confidence.' Tori shrugged. 'It's not the same without her.'

Patrick smiled as he sat at the desk beside her. 'I agree.'

Should she tell him? If anyone cared as much about Sarah as she did, it was Patrick. She saw the attention he paid Sarah; the way he would gather up his courage to go and talk with her. Patrick definitely felt something for Sarah. And she instinctively knew she could trust him. But she wouldn't risk Patrick getting involved any more than he already had. For the first time in her life, Tori was relieved when it was time to go home. Usually school was a release; a hiding place for her, but not that day. Sarah was sick and she needed to get home.

The bell finally went. She shoved her books and pens into her school bag, threw it on her shoulder and rushed to the school gate.

'Victoria!'

She jumped as her mother appeared at her side. If only Mum would stop using her full name; the name listed on so many of her trophies but which made her feel sick to the stomach. She didn't feel like a 'Victoria'. She never had.

'What are you doing here?'

Her mother looked pale and stressed. 'The audition time has been moved forward. Quick, we need to get going.'

Tori hesitated, trying to control the thoughts racing through her mind. Something wasn't right. Why hadn't her mother looked at her? Why did she look edgy, frightened? Taking a deep breath, she rushed after her, wondering why the car engine was already running, the door left wide open.

Tori watched her mother throw herself into the driver's seat. Half lowering herself into the passenger seat she paused and glanced into the back. 'Where's Sarah?'

Her mother blinked fast. 'She's too sick to come. Quick, get in. Shut the door.'

Too sick to come? Sarah never came with them. Tori just wanted to know if Sarah was at home or somewhere else. Her mother was acting strangely.

'Is she very sick? Too sick to look after herself?'

Her mother said nothing, and Tori felt fear race through her.

'Mum, what's going on?'

'I told you. Now shut up and let's go.'

Her mother moved the car forward with such a start that Tori fell into the seat as the wheels skidded in the gravel. Her door swung shut and adrenaline raced through her. She wasn't safe. Something serious had happened. Without any more thought, she flung the door open and jumped. Intense pain coursed through her as she hit the ground and rolled a few times. She wanted to run, but couldn't move.

'Tori!' A voice called out her name, and she looked up to see Patrick running toward her. His expression showed his horror. Before he reached her, her mother had stopped the car, backed up and opened the back door. She dragged Tori to the car and shoved her in.

'Don't you dare try that again!' She slammed the door and screeched off. Tori saw Patrick try to open the door, and then bang on the boot. He then stood helplessly watching as the car left him behind.

Chapter Two

'Mum, I need a hospital.' Tori gritted her teeth as her mother tore through the streets with no concern for the road rules.

'You need a good slapping, that's what.'

'I'm bleeding.'

'Good. I hope you bleed to death.' Her mother didn't even glance in the rear vision mirror. She became stony quiet.

A sick feeling of dread rose up within Tori and she hated herself for it. She'd stopped herself feeling afraid for a long time. Now her mother had managed to break through her protective barrier. One thing she knew; they weren't on their way to a modelling audition.

Curled up in a ball, ignoring the pain the way she'd taught herself, she was unable to put aside the fear because this time the fear wasn't for herself, it was for Sarah.

She managed to keep herself in a state of nothingness as the minutes turned to hours. Her mother drove on. Finally, she stopped. If only she had the energy to run for it but her scraped legs and elbows had become stiff and her head was pounding. She needed to bide her time. Her main thoughts were of Sarah. What had happened to her? Was she really all right? Something inside told her she wasn't.

Wordlessly, she followed her mother's orders as a large jacket was thrown over her shoulders to hide her bleeding arms.

She forced one aching leg in front of the other as they made their way into a city hotel. No one seemed to look in their direction. Why wouldn't they look at her? It was just like all those times at the auditions when other children's parents would walk past and she would wish that just one of them would realise what was going on and rescue her.

'This is your room.'

Tori looked at her mother's hard, cold face and then around the room they'd entered. She limped to the bed and lay there for several minutes, exhausted and hungry. She heard her mother getting some food in the adjoining room, but knew better than to ask for some. Then came the soft sound of the bar fridge opening and closing and the clinking of a bottle being opened.

Finally, all was quiet and Tori moved to the window. They were several stories up, and there was no escape. The window didn't open.

It was then it hit her. They were on the run.

The quiet tick of the clock mocked her speeding heartbeat and slowed the endless hours until midnight. Surely it was safe to move now? With a quiet groan she stood, straightening her stiff joints and frowning as fresh blood seeped from her elbow. She limped forward, pain searing her scraped skin with every move. She glanced at her elbow. She probably needed stitches. Intense pain ran through it and the agony she felt when she moved caused her to grit her teeth. Something was going on. Normally her mother would have had the cut seen to immediately. Unlike with Sarah, she never risked letting her 'model' daughter become scarred. It could cost her everything.

Tori opened the connecting door to a familiar sight. Her mother lay on the lounge, a bottle of alcohol beside her. But she was awake and tears rolled down her cheeks. She turned red eyes to Tori.

'I killed her.'

The words chilled Tori to the bone. 'Who?'

Her mother's weeping intensified. 'Sarah, of course. I didn't mean to, but she just made me so … so angry.'

Tori gasped, longing with all her heart to lash out at her mother, but knowing the safest thing to do was escape.

'It's no good running.' Her mother suddenly let out a laugh, the tears stopping abruptly. 'I can see the fear in your eyes. You know I'll find you wherever you go. And they'll never believe a girl like you. Go back to your room.'

Quietly, Tori did as he was told but her mind raced. In a moment of panic she shut the door and flicked the lock into place. She had to get to Sarah! But how? Painfully moving to the window, she looked way down to the street below. It was dark but she could make out a ledge just outside. With the adrenaline working through her body, she believed she could climb out there onto the ledge even with her arm the way it was. But the window would need to be broken.

She glanced around the room, then opened the top drawer. A heavy book sat there. *Gideon's Bible*, she read, and felt hope surge through her. This should work. Lifting it carefully, she took a step back, gripped it with all her might and threw it with force at the window. It thumped against the glass then fell to the floor.

Tori's eyes flew around the room. A chair. It had to work. Lifting it with both hands, she moaned as pain shot threw her arm. She used the pain to give her strength, stepping back, then charging at the window. The sound of glass breaking shattered the night and cool air rushed in.

Using the chair legs, she scraped the glass from the window sill to clear her way. The edge was still rough so she picked up the Bible from the floor and rested it on the sill. A scream of rage came through the door as her mother rattled the doorknob. Tori shut out the noise and set her focus on escape. Fear drove her on as she carefully knelt on the Bible then stepped out onto the ledge, refusing to look far below to the ground. Her hands shook but she clung with every bit of strength she could muster.

From one window ledge to the next she travelled until finally she came to a room where the curtains were open and the light was on. Holding tightly to the ledge with one hand, fingers now white and sweaty, she reached up and knocked on the window. The people in the room immediately looked up and their mouths dropped open. They ran around in confusion for a moment, and then one came to the window.

'We'll get you some help. Hold on.'

Relieved, Tori nodded at the man but forced herself not to relax. She needed to continue holding on and focusing on the room of light before her. Her arms were getting tired, stretched out above her and clinging to the ledge. The muscles in her shoulders were screaming at her. Her elbow was bleeding profusely and the blood was now running down it. Some of it splashed onto her forehead and dripped into her eyes. Should she just let go? Let it all be over?

'Don't give up! They're coming.'

The man again. His promise reminded her of Sarah. She couldn't give up, for Sarah's sake.

Finally she heard a siren and caught the reflection of flashing lights in the window. She glanced below and saw the people gathered around on the ground. All were encouraging her to keep going.

Emergency workers cut the pane of glass from the window and pulled her safely inside. Dazed and confused, she allowed the paramedics to check her over and settle her onto the stretcher before she was taken down in the elevator and lifted safely into an ambulance.

'Sarah,' was all she could whisper before they gave her pain relief and she fell into a deep sleep.

No one was around when Tori awoke in the hospital bed, arm stitched and bandaged, scraped legs treated. An emergency buzzer sounded so loudly through the ward she wanted to cover her ears.

One nurse called to another. 'It's the lady with the twins. Where's the doctor?'

'It's Rachel Clements,' another nurse called as she rushed past.

Tori watched in amazement as doctors and nurses seemed to come out of the walls, all racing full speed to a room down the hall. She had to get out of there. She wasn't safe. Her mother had killed Sarah and she could kill her too. This was her opportunity. Quietly, she crept from the room and made her way down the corridor and out the front door. Despite the pain in her body, she began to run.

***

The jackhammer lay on its side, lifeless for the moment. The sun beat down on the concrete, creating a steamy haze on the partially finished road base. Storm's eyes slid closed as he blocked out the chatter of sweaty workers going on around him. How could the day pretend nothing out of the ordinary was happening when his phone had just told him otherwise? The words of the text went over and over in his mind. *Rachel in surgery. Not looking good.*

Not looking good for who? Rachel? The unborn twins? He opened his eyes and glared into the sun. How dare it be shining right now?

'Whatcha doin', boy? Dreaming of a girl?'

Storm's head jerked toward the worker sitting calmly on his esky and munching on a sandwich. His eyes scanned the other grinning faces.

'No.'

'Praying your facial hair will grow so you can be a man like me?'

That came from the scruffy one with the unkempt beard. Storm gave him a sneering glance, unconsciously raising a hand to his own bristled cheek. He hadn't bothered shaving that morning.

One of the workers stood, throwing his rubbish into the nearby bin. 'How about a competition, guys? Whoever can get their beard to touch the ground first wins.'

'Easy. I win already.' The bearded man dropped to his knees, leaned forward and ran his whiskers through the dust. Storm shook his head in disgust while the other men hooted with laughter. So childish and shallow. He wanted nothing to do with their empty lives. And yet, there he was, working with them by day, sleeping by them at night.

He stood, scrunching his empty sandwich bag into a tight ball in his fist, and headed to his caravan. He was tired of all of it. Tired of this boring existence, but also angry at … at what? The drama? Of the threat on his sister-in-law's life? He slammed his caravan door shut and glanced at the newspaper sitting on his table. A photo of a model gazed back at him. She was beautiful, just like his own sister Misty had been before … before he scarred her for life.

He flipped the newspaper over, pushing the memory aside and glancing again at his phone screen. The waiting was driving him crazy, but he wouldn't let anyone know that. There was no way he was going to ask what was going on. He had no right to know.

***

Rachel's eyelids fluttered open. It was as though the cloud over her eyes cleared and she was looking into a hospital room, stark and empty. Then she turned to find herself gazing into a familiar face, and yet at the same time, one she could not place in her memory. It was a handsome face. Well defined, strong and determined. Yet those dark eyes were filled with a mixture of sorrow and hope that touched her heart. She felt tears begin to form and swallowed them back. Before her eyes swam a picture she presumed was a memory.

This man, several years younger, was riding a magnificent horse. He rode with an ease and grace that had her catching her breath. Then he stood on the back of the creature, his smile poised and confident.

Prince.

She hadn't realised she spoke the name aloud until he smiled.

'Prince?' she whispered again.

'I'm here, my Rachel.'

Confusion clouded her mind. His tone was tender, his eyes speaking of a love she could not understand. My Rachel? The term of endearment frightened her more than anything.

She tried to sit up but pain struck her abdomen. 'What am I doing here?'

Hope drained from Prince's eyes as they flew to the other person in the room. Rachel had not noticed her until then.

Grandma.

'You've had twins, Rachel.' Her grandmother came to her side. 'Congratulations.'

'Seton and Blythe, just like we planned.' Prince was smiling gently, but concern still shadowed his dark eyes.

Rachel gasped. She must be having a dream. She'd had a crush on Prince Clements ever since the handsome circus boy had arrived at her school, but his lack of faith in God had made her keep her distance. She would never marry anyone who didn't believe like she did.

Lord God, this is all wrong. Please wake me up. Yet she didn't really want to wake up. Prince's smile. The indication he loved her … She wanted to say something but no words would come. That was normal for her dreams. Some people had nightmares where they couldn't run. In her nightmares she couldn't speak.

'Rachel?' She heard Prince's voice so close it seemed real. But she didn't even try to answer. She had had enough of this confusing dream.

Chapter Three

Tori kept running. She didn't know where, she just knew something within was driving her. She needed to escape the awful words she had heard from her mother. She needed to escape the world of expectation; of cruelty and selfish gain. Once there had been Sarah—Sarah calling her to stay, giving her a reason to keep going. But now there was nothing. No one. Victoria Seeth only lived because she hadn't stopped breathing.

She ran through the night, through the unfamiliar streets with darkness chasing her. There had to be a place to go, some place she could finally call home. But what was a home without Sarah?

'I'm living in a nightmare!' She gasped for breath. 'Only I can never run in my nightmares. Why can I still run?'

***

Rachel was waking again. Pain tore across her abdomen. This was no dream. This was real.

'Rachel, you've had a caesarean and you have a beautiful baby boy and girl.'

Her head jarred as she stared at the female doctor in the room.

Of course. Her twins. When the contractions began she'd been scared she was going to lose them. She'd begged God with every gasping breath to spare them; to allow her to hold them alive and well in her arms. She was desperate to see them. Every part of her ached with longing because they were not there in her arms.

'Can I see them?'

The doctor sat on the edge of the bed and smiled in understanding at her desperation. 'Yes, we'll take you to the special care nursery as soon as we can. Right now you need to rest.'

That was easy to say but not easy to do. Adrenaline rushed through her and emotion overwhelmed her at the thought of her little babies there in the special care nursery.

'I'll come and see you soon and you'll be able to see your babies,' the doctor promised, 'but right now I need to let your husband know you're awake.'

Prince! Her husband of only two months. Rachel glanced down at her left hand, forgetting for a moment that she hadn't been able to wear her wedding ring at the end of her pregnancy. Her hands had swelled too much to get it on. She remembered the day Prince had slid that ring onto her finger with the promise that though they had begun their relationship the wrong way, with God's help they would continue it the right way.

Footsteps sounded down the hall and Rachel heard a voice that stirred up both excitement and joy within her. He was coming.

'They're doing okay,' she heard him telling the person who was asking but he sounded distracted. She knew he was as keen to see her as she was to see him.

'Rachel?' He looked hesitant as he approached the bed. She savoured his appearance; his dark good looks and short, wavy hair. The strong, sure way he walked and the magnetic eyes that looked so tenderly into her own.

'Are the twins here, Prince?' Her eyes widened in wonder. 'Are they really here?'

She saw the way he nodded and breathed a deep sigh of relief. 'Rachel, welcome back!'

Without thought she reached out to him, but fell back with a gasp of pain as the stitches pulled. His expression clouded with worry.

'I'm okay.' She managed a laugh. 'Just give me a hug, because I can't come to you.'

He smiled, the smile that always set her heart beating faster and affected her somewhere deep down inside. His arms came around her gently, as though he were afraid to hurt her.

'I was worried.' He chewed his lower lip, looking deeply into her eyes. 'I thought I might lose all of you.'

This amazing man she had only dreamed of loving as a teenager was worried about her. She glanced down at the finger her wedding ring was normally on. He loved her. And they had twins.

Oh God, I am so blessed! Rachel wondered why she was crying. Tears coursed down her face.

'Hey, it's okay.' Prince pulled her head onto his shoulder and stroked her hair. 'Everything's okay now.'

She knew it was. God had blessed her way beyond what she deserved. She glanced around the room. This wasn't the public section of the hospital.

'Prince, where am I?'

He smiled. 'They moved you and the twins to the private. Better care here.'

Her eyes widened. They couldn't afford private health cover. Prince was just a uni student and she hadn't been able to teach piano for a month, now. Worries crowded in but Prince held her closer, seeming to read her thoughts. 'Don't worry. It's covered. I have so much to tell you. We are so blessed, Rach.'

She looked up at him. His face was alive with excitement and his eyes danced. 'We've been offered a job.'

'A job? What do you mean *we*?'

'I met some people while you were out of it, and the doctors were delivering the twins. They're Christians and they were in the hospital chapel. I went there to pray for you and the twins. I thought we were going to lose you and I felt so helpless, but they prayed with me. We got talking and oh Rach, if we accept the job I finally get to use my media training! And even all my years in the circus, learning to perform in front of people … I think God's been preparing me for this job all along.'

Rachel loved the way his eyes shone with joy and she couldn't help chuckling at his delight. 'So what's the job? Tell me!'

'They want us to be the face of their church.'

She didn't want to appear stupid, but she had no idea what that meant. Instead, she asked, 'What church?'

'The Happy Kingdom Church. Have you heard of it?'

Rachel frowned, trying to remember. She wasn't sure.

'It's a fairly new church, but I think they believe the same as us. Anyway, they want us to be their representatives to the media. You and I and the twins will be on the cover of their magazines and brochures, we'll be in their television ads …'

It was there Rachel laughed put up a hand to stop him. 'Hold on, Prince. I'm not a model. I've got no training in media. And we don't even know what the church believes.'

Prince merely grinned at her. 'No, not yet, but we've been praying about a new church since we moved here. It seems like this might be the one. But get this. They said they'll pay me to work in ministry with them first, to get to know them. I will help deliver supplies to the homeless, and be a part of their ministry team and get paid good money for it. In fact, such good money I can hardly believe it's for real.'

'And what if we find we don't believe the same as them or support what they stand for?'

'Then we back out. But if we don't, our pay goes up even more. It's big money, Rach, and we'd be set for life.'

Rachel studied him, her mind whirling. He was so excited. It did seem as though God had given them this job. It solved all their worries about money and how to provide for the twins and afford the large house they were renting. He pulled her close again.

'We're so blessed, Rach! God is looking out for us and providing for us in ways I could never have thought up in my wildest dreams.'

She nodded against him. *God loves us. He really does.*

***

Every sense was on high alert and Tori's heart leapt at the sound of wheels scraping metal. A train. That meant a station was nearby. And maybe a phone. She followed the sound, ducking through the shadows of the street, still breathing hard. Dizziness threatened to overwhelm her but she couldn't stop now.

The station was quiet apart from a guard and a few late night passengers. She scanned the platform. There it was. A public phone booth. She had no money, but she needed to ring home. A picture of the bible from the hotel room flashed through her mind. Her scripture teacher at school said God always answered prayer. She doubted he would listen to someone like her, but she had nothing to lose.

'God, I need there to be money in the change slot. Please.'

She slipped her fingers into the slot, pushing back the metal flap as she and Sarah had done so many times in the past. Her heart beat fast as her fingers touched smooth, cold metal. Nothing. For a moment she had truly expected something. Maybe a miracle would happen and the phone would work without money?

With unsteady hands she lifted the receiver. A loud clink came as a coin clattered into the change slot. Dazed, she stared at the gold coin now held between her shaking fingers. God had done it. He really had. But why? She was just Victoria Seeth, loser and failure. But this was for Sarah. God was smart enough to know Sarah was worth it.

She forced her fingers to work as she pressed the buttons of her home phone number. 'Please Sarah, pick up! You have to be there!'

Click. 'Hello?' She started at the deep male voice.

'Um, hello. Is Sarah there?'

There was noise in the background. Muffled voices, then the deep male voice again. 'Who am I speaking to?'

Tori hesitated, her heart beating twice its normal rhythm. What should she do?

Then she heard another voice in the background. A female voice. 'She had no pulse when we got here. The boy, Patrick, had been working on her for a while …'

'Hello. Hello?' The deep male voice was demanding her attention again. She dropped the phone as something inside her died. A train pulled into the station and without another thought, she dashed toward the open door and jumped on. She didn't really care if a guard caught her without a ticket. There was nothing to care about anymore. It was true. Sarah was dead.

The train moved off and station after station blurred by. Her throat stung but she stubbornly fixed her eyes the next station. Time to get off. Hopefully she would find a new home.

She wandered the streets in the early morning light. This place was too well looked after for her to be invisible. She would need to find somewhere before the town came to life. A few people had begun to arrive on the streets. She slunk into the shadows, trying to keep well hidden. She crept behind the bank building and into a side street which seemed old and uninhabited. And there it was. An old coffee shop out of the way and obviously empty. It still held a real estate sign in its window, but the sign was faded and spider webs hung across the doorway.

She tiptoed in, searching for signs of life. The layers of dust showed there had been none for some time. Her stomach rumbled but she knew the most important thing to do now was to sleep. She was too tired to search around for somewhere comfortable, so let herself fall onto the dusty carpet. Blackness came crowding in.

Chapter Four

Tori woke with a horrible headache and a stomach churning with hunger. She felt so lost and helpless that for a moment she entertained the idea of going to the police and allowing them to place her in a foster home. She had considered the option before, but had always concluded it was better to live through the situation she was in than to risk not being believed. Her mother was a skilled liar and there was no saying what she'd do if she was forced to go back to her.

And yet, Tori wondered if anything could be worse than living alone, homeless, hungry and in emotional agony.

First she had to find some food. She stepped out onto the verandah of the coffee shop, glancing in each direction before moving down the street. She had no idea how to feed herself. The only option was to steal, but she wasn't sure how to go about that. Her arm was throbbing again, despite being so well stitched, and her scraped legs felt stiff. She had no choice. It was time to find a police station.

She searched the streets, still keeping to herself and avoiding people's curious stares. And then she saw it. The morning papers with her picture splashed across the front.

'Child model becomes murderer.'

Tori gasped as she stared at her own face pictured at her last modelling shoot and the face of her mother on the front page.

Under the picture of her mother were her mother's words, 'I came home to find Sarah lying on the floor …'

Heart thundering in her chest, Tori scanned the words.

'Ms Seeth said she only wanted to help Victoria. When she realised what her daughter had done, she tried to help her escape. Ms Seeth reported that her daughter then allegedly turned on her before escaping out the window of a hotel room. She was taken to hospital with injuries to her arms, but fled before police could interview her.'

Tori stopped reading. She felt sick to the stomach. The police would be after her. There was no way she could live a normal life now. Her mother was an expert deceiver and Tori was way too tired to fight for the truth. She needed to learn how to be homeless.

***

Storm threw down the newspaper he had been reading and glared at the men around him. All he wanted was a bit of peace in his lunch break but these guys couldn't mind their own business.

'Who is she?' the older guy Storm hadn't bothered to get to know asked, turning his head on an angle to look more closely at the cover picture.

Storm shuffled irritably on the esky he was sitting on. 'If you'd given me a chance to read in peace I might be able to tell you.'

He grinned. 'Snappy today, aren't we?

'He's always snappy. Needs a girl, if you ask me.'

Storm sneered at the one they called Trooper and flipped his thumb toward the newspaper. 'Not that kind of girl. She's a murderer.'

'Murderer?' Trooper snatched up the paper. 'No way. No girl who looks like that could be a killer.'

Storm grabbed the paper back. 'Don't make it grubby.'

Most of the men laughed, but the older guy glared at him beneath grey, bushy eyebrows. 'Bit of an upstart, aren't you? Think you're too good for us, too good for this job.'

Storm didn't answer as he waved smoke from one of the worker's cigarettes away from his face. He knew he was too good for the job. He had been a circus stunt rider in his childhood and early teen years. Working on the roads didn't match up in any way. But it was a job and it had been the only way his father would let him get out of school. It was also the only way he could get away from all the emotion and drama in his family. He wanted a quiet, predictable life.

With a grunt, he headed to his van. Let the guys talk about him. He didn't care.

He shut the door behind him and glanced again at the paper. He could understand what made a girl want to kill. He'd wanted to kill a few people in his time too. Anything to get rid of the rage building up inside him, increasing every day. It didn't help that his sister-in-law had somehow wound her way into his heart and then threatened to die. But she had ended up being fine. And her babies were too. He'd wasted emotion on drama and it had all come to nothing. He wasn't about to let himself be that weak again any time soon.

***

'Are you ready?'

Rachel nodded at the wardsman at the end of her bed. She could see her babies now. She'd looked after her baby brother for years, but this was different. These babies were hers. She swallowed hard. 'I'm ready.'

Once settled in the wheelchair, anticipation filled her. The wardsman pushed her forward and she looked straight ahead, desperate to go faster, to get to her children.

The wardsman pressed a button, then waited until two large double doors slid open. Then she was in the special care nursery—the place she would first meet her son and daughter.

Prince was at the other end of the room, standing beside two humidicribs and gazing into them. Rachel's eyes locked on those cribs. They looked like glass coffins. Machines beeped all around and she wanted to cover her ears. But then Prince turned and saw her. He slowly smiled the smile that first captured her heart. He stepped aside as she was wheeled up beside him.

'Meet Seton and Blythe.'

She couldn't speak as she gazed at the two tiny little people in their cribs with tubes and thin wires attached to white patches on their fragile little bodies.

'They're doing well.' A nurse breezed over from the other side of the room. She smiled down at Rachel. 'You must be Mum.'

Rachel just nodded.

'Seton had a bit of breathing trouble so that tube in his mouth is attached to this machine which is breathing for him. He should be fine once his lungs are a bit more developed.'

Rachel stared at the little boy with the name tag above him. So that was Seton.

'Blythe is strong and quite a little character. She has a lot of energy for such tiny little girl.'

Rachel's heart began to respond. These truly were two tiny little people, each with their own personalities and souls. She recognised the dark hair and olive complexion. For some reason she had expected them to be light and fair like herself and her little brother, but these babies resembled Prince. These fragile, wrinkled children with squinting eyes were hers.

'Can I touch them?' Her voice came out in a whisper.

The nurse nodded and brought some sanitising gel to wash her hands. She was unable to nurse Seton yet, but when Prince placed little Blythe in her arms, she knew everything would be okay. It was still hard to believe this little baby was hers, but whatever it took she would protect and care for these children with everything she had.

She gazed down at the bundle in her arms for several minutes and Prince allowed her the silence. She touched the soft skin gently and savoured the baby smell. She would have liked to stay that way all day, but the phone in the nursery rang, and a nurse called across to her.

'You have a visitor waiting for you back at the ward.'

She nodded and held Blythe closer for a moment before allowing Prince to take her from her arms.

'Annoying visitors!' Prince laughed at her pained expression and nudged her. 'Don't you hate it when people care enough to come and see you in hospital?'

She grinned and went to give him a playful poke but remembered her stitches just in time. Any sudden movement pulled. She couldn't help her chuckle when the nurse took Blythe from Prince's arms and pushed him toward her.

'You're going too, Daddy Clements. The wardsman has left and can't take her back right now. Looks like it's up to you.'

He gave a good-natured grin and a shrug. 'And I thought the hard work was going to be looking after the babies, not my wife!'

A smile tugged at the corners of Rachel's mouth as she looked up into his eyes. She could honestly say she had never loved him more than she did just then. Every part of her being was filled with gratitude and joy.

It was clear Prince didn't feel put out that he had to take her back to her room. In fact, he thoroughly enjoyed himself. At every corner he pretended to screech the wheelchair to a stop, making comments about driving without a license and the chair being out of control. He muttered that he'd prefer to guide a horse around because they at least responded to instructions. Rachel laughed at his playfulness, knowing it was good for him to relieve the tension of the past few days. Her thoughts as they came back into the ward were that nothing would be the same again.

She was right.

Her eyes were drawn to the visitor waiting in her room and

she gasped. 'Kylie!'

Her cousin grinned from ear to ear. 'So you're a mum already? How on earth did that happen?'

She frowned. 'I thought you were still in Ireland!'

'I was.' Kylie tossed her pretty head and glanced toward Prince. 'But your husband contacted me and suggested you guys might be able to do with some help over the next few months. Especially now that he might be starting a new job.'

'What about your boyfriend in Ireland?

She shrugged. 'We're taking a break from each other. We weren't that serious.'

Rachel looked to Prince, feeling her heart sink. There had always been a spark between Prince and Kylie, one that had left her with mixed feelings. She loved her cousin but she also loved Prince. She hated to think of her cousin as competition.

You're married now, she reminded herself. *There's nothing to compete for.*

Yet as Kylie gave Prince an enthusiastic hug and congratulated him on becoming a father, she wished her cousin had left out the hug. And she wished Prince hadn't looked so pleased to see her.

***

The babies were three days old and Rachel was tired of hospital. She was tired of waiting for visitors to come and then waiting for them to go so she could see Seton and Blythe. She was tired of competing with Kylie for Prince's attention, she was tired of the hospital food, the hospital noises and smells. She was tired, full stop.

'Hey, what's wrong?' Kylie bounced into the room, Prince not far behind. She sat on the bed, leaving no room for Prince to bend down and give his usual good morning kiss. Rachel tried to stop the tears filling her eyes, but didn't succeed.

'I don't know. I'm just a bit down, I guess.'

Prince came to the other side of the bed and took her hand,

looking deep into her eyes. 'It's the day three and four blues.' There was understanding and comfort there.

'The what?' Kylie asked, but Rachel knew what he was talking about. They had been warned about the post-pregnancy hormones that often left mothers feeling overwhelmed after a few days.

'I just want to go home.' A tear spilled down her cheek.

He nodded. 'I want you home too.' He moved closer, and his voice came out soft and full of meaning. 'I'm missing you.'

She understood the yearning in his eyes and her hand tightened around his.

'The doctor said maybe tomorrow.'

Her eyes filled with tears again. 'But he said Seton will have to stay. How can we leave him here all by himself?'

He bit his lip and she knew he felt the same.

'Hey,' Kylie interrupted, bouncing up again, 'They give them the best care here. Enjoy the time without him. Seton will be waking you up at dawn for the next twenty years. Don't wish it on yourself any sooner than you have to.'

Both Prince and Rachel swung around to Kylie and Rachel finally let out a small laugh. 'Wait until you have a baby, then you'll understand.'

Kylie stepped back, both hands up as though warding off the idea. 'No, that's not the life for me!' She threw her thumb in Prince's direction. 'Why do you think I dumped him all those years ago?'

Prince laughed, but his laugh was hollow and Rachel frowned. Why did she have to bring that up? It was true Kylie had ended their relationship when she'd discovered Prince had a daughter, but this wasn't about his past mistakes. However, she didn't seem to realise she'd said the wrong thing and continued talking about the woes of having children.

When she left the room to go outside for a smoke, Rachel's eyes met with Prince's. 'What are we going to do?'

'Do? About what?' He frowned in puzzlement.

'About Kylie?'

His eyes widened. 'You don't like having her around?'

She saw the way he tried to understand, concern filling his dark eyes, and she wondered whether or not to voice her fears. He'd asked Kylie to come because he had wanted to help her. How could she tell him she wasn't happy about it? He was waiting.

'She doesn't even like children, Prince.'

He chuckled. 'That's what she wants us to believe. But she likes you, and that's why I asked her.'

'What about her smoking? What about when Seton comes home?'

His eyes widened for a moment as he caught on. Then his expression became stern. 'She'll just have to smoke outside.'

She gave him a look, then grinned. 'Are you going to tell her or am I?'

He bit his lower lip, a smile tugging at his mouth. 'Good point.'

'So what are we going to do?'

He stood and paced the room for a few moments, hands in pockets. Then he turned back to her. 'We'll see how it goes. Let's at least wait and pray about if I should take this new job or not. We'll talk about it more when we get home.'

She let out a slow breath. Fair enough. She should see how it went before sending her cousin packing. They had been as close as sisters in the past, but very different. Maybe Kylie was just who she needed to help her through the next few months.

However, she still couldn't help feeling annoyed that she had to share Prince and her babies with someone else.

Lord, please give me the right attitude. And help me look after my son and daughter.

Peace filled her as she prayed. She had cared for her baby brother and taken on the role of caregiver when her parents had been killed overseas. She had only been sixteen but she had managed. She would be able to care for her twins.

Chapter Five

Tori awoke to the sound of raised voices.

'You dobbed me in,' one hooded teen screamed at another, his fist raised.

'I didn't do nothin'. I couldn't care less what you buy or sell.' The other kid backed off and Tori sighed, pulling her jumper over her head. Sleeping in the park surrounded by other homeless kids gave her a sense of security but didn't give her refreshing sleep.

'Better get used to it, Aura,' a voice said at her side.

She pulled her jumper back down and looked into the eyes of the one they called Trojan. She still hadn't worked out if Trojan was a boy or a girl. Suddenly she had an urge to know. She sat up and looked into Trojan's hardened eyes. 'What's your real name?'

The teen let out a laugh. 'Not tellin' you, kid, just like you're not tellin' me yours. None of us street kids use our real names. Safer that way.'

Tori nodded, wondering how many of them were on the run from the law like she was. The drug use was rampant, but only the one called Kenny seemed to be a real dealer.

Her stomach grumbled and the pinch tightened deep inside. Despite this being her first time homeless, the feeling wasn't new. One of her mother's most common punishments was to deny food. The fights amongst the street kids didn't bother her either; she had seen worse in her own home. The lack of love suited her too. She'd allowed herself to love, then seen the ones she loved turn on her or be killed. She wasn't going to make that mistake again, and so watching the fights, the stabbings and the arguments of the homeless was like watching a movie.

She knew she was disconnected from everything and she didn't care. Emotions were way too dangerous and true love and hope were a myth. Fear was a weakness she couldn't afford to entertain.

She glanced at the sleeping forms hidden in their sleeping bags around her. Kenny, Trojan, Skeeter and Lana had taken her under their wing. They hadn't asked her name, just called her Aura. Kenny said it was because of the aura of hardness around her. Tori knew she had put a protective barrier around herself, but no one seemed to mind and she felt safer that way. She also felt relief in the anonymity the name 'Aura' gave her.

She no longer looked anything like the model she used to be. Nobody would guess she was the wanted Victoria Seeth. She was too skinny, too ragged, she never smiled and her hair was a tangled mess. Even her skin showed signs of wear it never had before. Tori's new life suited her to a tee … if it could be called a life.

***

Rachel stood watching as Prince carefully buckled baby Blythe into her car seat. She glanced longingly over at the other side of the car to Seton's empty baby seat. It seemed wrong to be bringing one home and not the other, but Seton wasn't strong enough yet.

Prince straightened and turned, smiling into her eyes and causing her to catch her breath. He was not in his usual casual jeans and tee-shirt, but dressed in smart suit trousers and a tailored shirt. He had done his first trial shift at the Happy Kingdom Church and they had provided him with some nice clothes. Rachel found it endearing that he had dressed up for this special occasion. And it *was* special. Even Storm had come to the hospital to see them on their way, though she wasn't sure why. He stood beside her, watching with his usual expression of distaste.

Blythe let out a tiny sound that reminded Rachel of a kitten. She smiled, looking forward to the day her daughter would let out a strong, healthy cry.

'She's very wrinkled.' Storm was now looking in through the car window. Trust Prince's brother to speak his mind. There was no way he would pretend he thought the baby was cute and all the things you were supposed to say.

Prince grinned at his brother. 'She'll iron out in the wash.'

'Prince!' Rachel tried not to laugh, but it bubbled up inside her and burst out.

'Ow,' she moaned, holding her stomach. The wound still pulled.

'No coughing or laughing, remember?' Storm's voice was gruff, his look fierce.

'Don't be funny, then.'

Storm's mouth twitched and his frown now seemed forced. 'It wasn't me. Talk to your precious husband about it.'

'I'm sorry.' Prince tried to look repentant but failed. 'I don't see what was so funny, anyway.'

She smiled and shook her head. 'For a start, it's a terrible thing to say about a baby, but you were mixing up two sayings. It's either, it will all come out in the wash, or it'll all iron out. Ironing and washing are two separate things.'

She giggled again while he shrugged. 'I grew up in the circus. I'm not supposed to know that kind of thing.'

Storm nodded. 'Yeah, don't blame him for his ignorance. Just don't let him bath the baby. And hide your iron.'

Another giggle erupted and she held her stomach but managed not to laugh out loud. 'You two. The sooner you're separated the better. Are we ready to go?'

Storm stepped back from the car, his hands raised. 'Okay, okay. I've got things to do anyway.'

She gave him an affectionate smile and went to hug him, but he pulled away. Instead, she gave him a pat on the shoulder. 'Thanks for coming, Storm. It means a lot.'

He merely grunted. 'Had to see the twins, didn't I? Everyone's going on about them like they're amazing and asking me what I think of them. Now I've had a proper look without that glass crib thing all around them I can tell them.'

Prince closed the car door and gave his brother a look. 'What will you tell them?' He put up a hand. 'Actually, I don't want to know. You can keep your opinions to yourself. But thanks for coming, Storm. We do appreciate it. Really.'

Storm shrugged and looked anywhere but at his brother. 'Well, as I said, I'd better go.' He turned and stalked away.

Rachel looked at her husband. 'He can't really be that annoyed with everyone and everything all the time, can he?'

Prince pursed his lips for a moment. 'I don't know. If not, he's a pretty good actor.' Then he grinned. 'But let's forget about Storm. We're taking our daughter home, Rachel.' He moved over and opened her door, waiting until she carefully lowered herself into the seat. She reached for the handle and winced. Prince gave her hand a gentle tap.

'My job. At least until you're all healed.'

She screwed up her nose, but he bent down until his eyes were level with hers.

'Deal?' The look in his dark eyes melted her the way it always had. 'Okay, deal.' He went to stand up but she reached for his hand. 'Thank you.'

Her words were filled with meaning and he smiled slowly. 'My pleasure.'

Then he raced around to the driver's side of the car and jumped in. 'Home we go.'

Rachel looked over at him. The attraction she felt was so strong it scared her. Because if she found him so appealing, Kylie would too. Prince Clements had merely grown better looking as he matured. Kylie had only known him as a reckless, brazen teenager who was capable of doing whatever he set out to do. Now he was a godly, tender-hearted man any woman would fall for if given the chance. And if Kylie lived with them she would certainly be given the chance. 'I still don't know if it's best for Kylie to live with us.'

Prince reached to put a hand on hers for a moment before returning it to the steering wheel. 'The hospital recommended we get help. I'm sorry I couldn't ask you at the time. But I do think we'll need someone through the night, at least until you're better. And if we take up this job, we'll need help.'

She bit her lip, unsure what to think. It was true they had been worried about money and providing for the twins, but she had always pictured her and Prince caring for them together at home.

'If you take the job, will you be able to finish uni?'

He nodded. 'They said I can. It will mean extra hours away from you and the babies.' He glanced her way, looking troubled. 'So if you'd prefer I didn't take up the job, we will work out a way to make it. But it does kind of seem like God's provision for us.'

She agreed. It did. It was worth following up, anyway. The money was too good to ignore. She studied Prince and saw the strain in his face. He was right that having Kylie around would be a big help. And she knew he had no hidden motives. It must have been so hard for him. He'd expected her to come home from the hospital healthy and strong, able to care for two little babies. Instead, he was bringing home just one of their children and a wife recovering from major surgery.

On top of that, they would be making daily trips to the hospital to see little Seton. Without help, he would have to shoulder most of the responsibility and housework for six weeks. Maybe Kylie was actually a gift. 'It's okay. Having Kylie will make things easier. And I think you should at least trial the job, get to know the people and the church.'

His shoulders visibly relaxed at her words and she regretted voicing her concerns. He was just trying to help. She needed to accept his choices with a grateful heart.

They pulled into their driveway and he gave her a tender look as he turned off the ignition. Home. She gave him a full, complete smile.

'We're home, little one!' Prince said as he carefully lifted the sleeping Blythe from the baby capsule. 'And you're not even awake to see it. Just like your mother, aren't you?'

Rachel's look was quizzical. 'She is?'

He grinned. 'Yeah, you slept through the most important moment; their birth.'

She screwed up her nose. 'I didn't have much choice in it. Those doctors had me out to it pretty quickly once they thought trouble was coming.'

'Trouble, hey? You think they're going to be trouble?'

She laughed. 'They look just like you. What do you think?'

He laughed too, and she savoured the sound. He settled the baby in his arms and looked across the top of the car at her.

'I think, Rachel, that you're more than enough trouble for all of us.'

She grinned back, not bothering to retaliate. Her heart swelled with gratefulness. *Thanks God, for Prince. Thanks for my children. Please help me be a good mother!*

It wasn't until she stepped into the house and Blythe began to fuss that the enormity of the task hit her. Kylie was there, wanting to say hello and show her how she had set up the babies' room, Prince was asking her where to put the bag of nappies they'd brought home from the hospital, and Blythe's cry was weak but demanding.

'I think she needs a feed.' Rachel glanced from Prince to Kylie and suddenly felt alone. Kylie and Prince were well-meaning, but neither of them had experience with babies. If only her mother were still alive to help.

They stood looking at her, as though waiting for her to take charge. With a deep breath, she sat down and reached her arms out for the baby.

Kylie sat down and watched. 'It's not like having a kitten or puppy, is it?'

Her brow flew up and Kylie's comment, but she knew what she meant. This wasn't fun. It was hard work and scary. This baby girl was dependent upon her to meet her every need. And soon there would be Seton to care for too. What if she failed?

Kylie moved toward her. 'Rachel, are you shaking?'

She shrugged as she tried to focus on feeding Blythe. 'Yeah, I guess so.'

'Are you okay?'

She nodded, wondering how she could ask Kylie to leave for a moment so she could get her bearings and focus on Blythe.

'You'll be okay. You always are. Whatever comes at you, you face it head on. What did Grandma always say about you?' She raised her eyes, trying to recall. 'That's it. Rachel has strength, dignity and integrity. Or something like that. Anyway, I know you'll get through this, just like you always do.'

Rachel looked up, then back down at Blythe, who was fussing again. She knew her cousin didn't believe in God and she'd always tried to be a good witness to her. Was her fear now setting a bad example? Surely she should be able to do this in God's strength. She let out a deep sigh. She was just too tired. Time to stop guessing what Kylie might be thinking.

'Want me to try settling her a bit?'

She looked up in surprise at Kylie's hopeful tone. 'Thanks.' She handed Blythe over. If she could just have a moment she would be able to relax enough to feed Blythe. But it was hard to even think while the baby was crying and wriggling. She watched as Kylie put the baby over her shoulder and began patting her back. How people could change! The carefree, bubbly Kylie was holding and rocking a baby as though it was the most natural thing in the world for her to do. And the unruly, brazen Prince Clements was now a devoted husband and father.

He walked into the room at that moment and his eyes danced. 'Won't be long till we have a house full! Imagine what it will be like once Sky and Paul live here too.'

Dismay filled Rachel at the thought of Prince's daughter and her own brother waiting to be taken into their home. They'd agreed to do that before the babies had been born and they were renting this large house so they could fit them all in. Sky's mother didn't care for her very well and they felt she needed a more stable influence, and she wanted to be there for her little brother too.

She couldn't think about them just now. She had a baby needing her almost every hour of the day and night. And she was so tired. With a deep breath she prayed for calm, then reached again for Blythe. The baby needed a feed.

***

'Rach, sorry to wake you, but there's someone I want you to meet.'

Prince's voice shook Rachel from her sleep. She tried to sit up. Her hand flew to stomach as the jarring movement shot pain through her surgery site.

'You all right?' Prince asked and it was then she realised with embarrassment that the visitors were already in the room. She had fallen asleep on the lounge and Prince had let the strangers in. Or were they strangers? She looked harder, blinking through sleepy eyes.

The man was around fifty with greying hair and a wide, friendly smile. He wore suit trousers and a smart, tailored shirt much like Prince was wearing that day. His wife was younger-looking and walked ahead of her husband with confidence and an air of authority. Jewellery dangled from her neck and wrists and her hair was tied up in a tight knot on top of her head.

'Hello, Rachel, I'm Deborah.' The woman bent down to give her a smothering hug. The diamond on her bracelet poked into Rachel's shoulder.

'And this is Parker,' Prince added when Deborah failed to introduce her husband. 'They are the couple I told you about from Happy Kingdom Church who have offered us the job. They were at the hospital while you were in theatre and the twins were being born. They prayed with me. And they laid hands on Seton just before he was healed.'

Rachel's eyes widened. She hadn't known Prince had let them in to the special care nursery to see the twins, nor that they had prayed for Seton. What was he healed from?

There was something about this couple she was uncomfortable with, but couldn't pinpoint it. 'Healed?'

He nodded. 'The doctors said he was in a pretty bad way and might not make it in that first hour, but after Deborah and Parker laid hands on him, he improved. And then you were moved to the private hospital.'

Rachel swallowed hard, wishing she could have been conscious when the twins were born. It was awful not being a part of something so important.

'So good to see baby Blythe is already home, just like we prayed,' Parker said, changing the subject and glancing to where Kylie now stood in the doorway, holding Blythe and giving the couple a curious look. Rachel reached her arms for her daughter, but Deborah stepped forward and took the baby from Kylie's arms. She began praying in a foreign tongue. Rachel stood quickly, ignoring the pain it brought to her wound as she came to Deborah's side.

'I need to feed her.' She spoke quietly but firmly.

Deborah paused only briefly before looking her in the eye. 'I can see you're not yet competent. You still have a spirit of fear and the baby can sense that. You go and get some rest and I'll settle her.'

Kylie's eyebrows flew to her hairline and Rachel gritted her teeth. Who did this woman think she was? A protective streak rushed through her and she held out her arms. 'She needs to be fed.'

Please, please God, make her give her back. I don't have the energy to fight!

Kylie came forward and firmly took Blythe from Deborah's arms, giving Rachel a look over the lady's shoulder. 'It's okay. I'm here to help Rachel.'

Deborah appeared ruffled but nodded. 'I'll pray for both of you, for your salvation and for the salvation of the little ones.'

Rachel could not have been more shocked, but Prince didn't argue as he thanked Parker and Deborah for coming and saw them out the door.

'The hide of them!' Kylie fumed as Rachel sat down, her head in her hands. It was all too overwhelming.

'Prince, what did she mean? Doesn't she know I'm a Christian?'

He looked uncomfortable for a moment, looking anywhere but at her.

'Prince?'

Finally he met her eyes. 'Well, obviously I told them we are. But maybe they do have some different views from ours.'

'Such as?'

'When I first met them in the hospital chapel I was a bit, well, emotional. I thought I would lose you. My prayers were having no effect. And then Deborah and Parker turned up. They said they had come to pray with me because God had led them to a family in great need. They said he wants to bless us richly.'

Rachel's eyes widened. 'The private hospital?'

'Yes, they prayed for it. They said God wanted you to have the best care.'

'Prayed for it or paid for it?'

Prince's eyebrows raised as though he hadn't thought of that. 'I don't know.'

'What did they pray for?'

He bit his lip. 'For a miracle, I guess. They were praying in another language. I'm not sure what they said, but I'd felt helpless until then. I can't explain it except to say I felt empowered and … well, I started praying in another language too. It's like God just took over my tongue, and here you all are, alive and well.'

Rachel's eyes filled with recognition. 'I've heard of people like them. They believe God wants us to all be rich and that you have to speak in tongues to be a Christian?'

He bit his lip, rubbing the back of his neck. 'Um, I'm not really sure. I think they did say something about it being the sign of being saved. And they did ask if you speak in tongues. I admitted you don't.'

She studied him. 'I think we're going to have to be careful, Prince.'

He didn't answer and at that point Kylie cut in with a harsh laugh.

'Who do you think you are, Prince, letting them think you're a Christian but Rachel's not? Rachel's more Christian than anyone else I've ever known! Her faith blows me away, even though I don't share it. And here are you, the bad boy of the school, the womaniser, the sinner who suddenly thinks he knows better in one day than Rachel had learned in years. Your pride is unbelievable!'

'I don't think I'm better than Rachel!' His hurt was evident in the shadow that passed through his eyes. 'I just didn't know how to explain it to them. I haven't been a Christian that long myself.'

Kylie glared at him. 'Well, I don't think you should take that stupid job if that's the way they think.'

Prince opened his mouth to retaliate but glanced at Rachel. She wished she could stop the tears filling her eyes and silently sliding down her cheeks. He closed his mouth and came to her. She allowed him to draw her close. She spoke into his shirt, the smart, quality shirt the visitors had provided for him.

'Sorry, Prince, but I don't think I'm ready for visitors yet.'

Kylie stood. 'Well I'm not ready for visitors like that, either!' She was getting worked up, waving her hands in the air. 'Can you believe anyone would take a baby from its mother like that?'

Rachel saw Prince's mouth twitch despite his obvious concern for her distress. 'Kylie, do you mind giving us a minute?'

Kylie stopped mid-rant, met his gaze and silently left the room.

Prince let out a sigh and half chuckle before turning to look directly at Rachel. 'Should I pull out of the job? Just say the word and I will. It's not worth it if it's going to cause stress.'

Rachel studied him for a moment, then looked down at Blythe. Prince had bought quality nappies for her this morning and she seemed a lot more comfortable and settled. They had also replaced the old, second-hand cots they had been given with brand new ones. They were now able to comfortably afford rent as well as care better for their twins.

'Let's wait a bit longer. We don't know for sure what they believe, yet. And if God has provided this job for us …' Her voice faded out. Had God provided it?

He bit his lip, looking unsure. 'They've asked me to go with them to the homeless shelter tonight, Rach, but I can pull out if you like. I told them you might need me here.'

She stiffened. And let them think she wasn't competent? That she was clingy and needed Prince every moment of the day and night?

'No, you go, Prince. I've got Kylie. She's not you, but she'll do for a few hours. But if you feel uncomfortable or anything doesn't feel right, remember you're free to pull out of the job any time you want.'

He smiled and warmth filled his eyes. 'I'll be back as soon

as I can, I promise. Parker said some of these poor homeless kids have nothing. '

He was right. Surely she could let her husband go out and share God's love with those who had so little? She loved him for wanting to. She gave him a warm smile. 'I love you.'

He brushed a kiss to her forehead. 'I love you too.'

Rachel was feeding Blythe again when Prince stepped into the room that evening. 'I'm heading off to the homeless shelter now. I'll be back as soon as I can.'

She grabbed his hand and looked him up and down. 'Another new outfit?'

He glanced down at his expensive looking clothes. 'Deborah and Parker gave them to me to wear tonight. Mine weren't suitable for the ministry work we're doing.'

She grinned at him. 'You always look pretty good to me. Surely you don't have to look like a rich man to reach the homeless?'

Prince gave her a thoughtful look before giving her another kiss and a last wave.

The door had only just closed when Blythe's weak cry came from the babies' room. Prince was right. Kylie would help.

Chapter Six

Tori was tired of fighting for survival. She couldn't go inside the homeless shelter where the staff kept an eye out for criminals and runaways, of which she was both. Instead, she and her group hung around, waiting for Kenny to deal drugs to provide money for them. Even there, Tori felt like a lower class human or an animal. Nothing could make her accept anything from these people.

'Quick, that weird church group are giving out blankets tonight!'

Tori heard the group calling her to join them and she was torn. Food she could resist for a time, but the nights were getting colder and the deep ache in her bones made her long for warmth. A blanket would help.

She inched forward and eyed the blanket. Memories flooded in. She felt like a little girl again—shivering, hiding under her blanket, hoping that somehow it would make her invisible. Hoping her mother wouldn't bother lifting it to strike her or hurl abuse. Jarred by the memory, she stepped back just as one of the women held out a grey woollen blanket. The woman's eyes narrowed and for a moment something in her eyes reminded Tori of her mother.

The challenge in the woman's eyes grew. 'I know it's not pretty, but beggars can't be choosers, can they?'

Tori's glanced down at herself. Yes, she was a beggar and she looked like one. But she could still make choices. No one could take free choice from her. She didn't *have* to take the blanket.

'Well?' The woman looked down her nose at her, and Tori wondered why a woman who seemed to despise her would bother to give her a blanket. She glanced at the name tag on the ample chest. Deborah. She didn't like her and she didn't like the name. But the blanket would make such a difference on cold nights. She warred within herself, trying to work out what to do. Finally, she caved. With trembling hands, she reached for the blanket, just as Deborah pulled it away and held it out to the next person in line.

Tori gritted her teeth. She was sure the woman had done that on purpose. Well, now Sarah was dead and she had nothing to lose. With lightning speed, she snatched a blanket from a pile on the ground and ran.

'Grab her!' Deborah's thundering voice rang out and all the homeless moved aside to let her through. They looked after their own.

But strong arms came around her, forcing her still. Fear paralysed her for a moment as Deborah raced over, followed by a group of well-dressed people from the church.

'What's going on?'

At the sound of her captor's deep but gentle voice, Tori looked up and her eyes widened. She was imprisoned in the arms of the most handsome man she had ever seen. Movie star was her first thought. She searched for his name tag. Prince. Strange name, but it suited him.

'She stole the blanket!' Deborah's bellowing voice made Tori want to block her ears but she couldn't move. She watched helplessly as Deborah reached for the blanket, gave it a rough shake, then glared into Tori's eyes.

'We're giving them away.' Prince's tone was puzzled. 'She's supposed to take it.'

Deborah took a step back. 'Yes, but not that way. She snatched it and ran.'

'She snatched a free blanket?'

Tori felt Prince's arms loosen around her as he asked the question. Deborah looked cornered and Tori could have hugged Prince. Instead, she grabbed another blanket from the ground and ran without looking back.

* * *

Rachel heard the car door and knew Prince was home and ready to drive them to the hospital to see Seton. She moved toward the change table with Blythe, pulling a nappy from the bag with more force than was necessary. It felt like she was changing or feeding baby Blythe every moment of the day. And once Seton came home from hospital and she no longer needed Prince to drive her, he would be working longer hours for the Happy Kingdom Church. That's if they decided to go ahead with the job. She liked the pay, but something about Deborah and Parker didn't sit right. She frowned at the mere thought of the overbearing couple. Last night, Prince had relayed the story of the homeless girl taking a free blanket and Deborah making a big fuss about it. It didn't make sense.

She's got control issues.

Rachel shook her head. That wasn't a nice thought to have about someone she hardly knew. She needed to at least give Deborah a chance and get to know her.

'How's it going?' Prince's voice came in her ear as he planted a kiss on her cheek. He then bent down to do the same to Blythe. His eyes widened. 'She gets bigger by the minute!'

Rachel nodded. If Prince took the job he would miss seeing so much of his children. They grew up so fast. She neatly smoothed the new nappy on and pulled Blythe's dress down over the top.

'She's been unsettled this morning. But so have I.'

Immediate concern filled his eyes as he picked up Blythe. 'Everything okay?'

'Deborah rang.'

48

His brows rose. 'For?'

'She wants me to come to the church prayer meeting tonight. And wanted to remind you about it.'

He frowned. 'I haven't forgotten. But I told her you need to be here for Blythe and that you're very tired.'

'She wants me to bring her.'

Prince shook his head, waiting for Rachel to pick up the nappy bag, then headed out to the car. Rachel followed.

'I don't think she has children.' Prince made the comment while locking the front door behind them and carefully balancing Blythe in his other arm.

Her thoughts exactly. 'What does she want from me, Prince?'

Prince's brows raised and he didn't answer until Blythe was buckled safely into her car seat and they were on their way.

'I think she wants a supermum, but we'll just have to let her know they don't exist.'

To Rachel's dismay, she felt her throat tighten and her eyes fill. 'I'd like to be one.' She wished the tears in her voice weren't so obvious.

She felt his warm hand rest on her arm for a moment before he returned it to the steering wheel. 'I don't want you to be one. It's you I want. I married you. So if Deborah can't handle that, that's her problem.'

'But this is your dream job, Prince. What if I let you down?'

He smiled. 'You won't. Relax. Let's just enjoy seeing Seton.'

Rachel took a deep breath. She had to stop worrying so much. Prince wasn't worried, so she shouldn't be either. God would direct them.

***

Prince looked around, wondering what to expect in his first Bible study in the Happy Kingdom Church. The group was small and he wondered how the church could afford to pay him so much.

49

Surely twenty people didn't tithe the amount he received?

'So how are things going with that wife of yours?'

Prince looked up as Deborah's question was directed to him. He hesitated. How much should he share with this group of relative strangers?

Parker leaned forward. 'Prince, we want to be able to support you and your family in prayer. That means being willing to be open so that we can pray informed prayers. You can trust us. We're your family here. Your brothers and sisters in Christ.'

Prince bit his lip. He didn't want to betray Rachel. 'She's tired a lot and a bit more emotional, but she's doing okay.'

'Do you think she has post-natal depression?'

The question came from another member of the group and he had to think. Was Rachel's lethargy normal? She had lost her sparkle, but who wouldn't when they were getting up all hours of the night to feed and settle a baby?

'I'm not sure.'

Deborah stood. 'We need to lay hands on her. We need to go around to your home.'

Prince was startled. 'Um, maybe not now. She said she's not really up to visitors.'

'Ah, it *is* depression.' Parker looked knowingly at him and many of the group nodded their heads in agreement. 'We need to fast for her. We can't give up until she is released from this vile scourge.'

Prince's heart beat faster. He reached for a mint sitting on the coffee table in front of him. 'I think she's okay, really. The doctor hasn't seemed worried.'

'No,' Deborah agreed, 'Because he's looking for physical illness. What Rachel has is spiritual. What is stopping her from coming here to join us? What is holding her back? I'll tell you. The devil knows that God has amazing plans for her and he wants to stop them. We must pray she will be released from his power and come.'

Prince raised his eyebrows, sucking on the mint and fiddling with the wrapper. He had been praying Rachel would feel up to coming in the right time. He had presumed it mustn't be God's time yet or that it wasn't best for her to come.

'God isn't going to work unless we pray with true, unwavering faith.' Deborah now stood up, speaking with passion, and all those in the group nodded their heads. Parker stood too, his eyes piercing as he looked around the circle. 'If anyone here has doubts, we need to pray against them and deal with that before we continue. We need to pray with power and authority!'

Prince wondered whether to speak out. He had doubts. He doubted Rachel's need was spiritual. He thought she just needed more sleep, more time. To his surprise, sudden energy surged through him with a startling ferocity before filling him with excitement and a sense of uninhibited power. He sat up straighter, resolved. He refused to be the reason she was suffering. He would believe. Rachel was going to be healed because he was going to pray in faith

'Let's pray for her.' His voice came out strong and loud, caught up in the moment. 'Let's release her in Jesus' name.'

A young woman who'd been introduced as Rebecca earlier in the evening spoke up. 'The problem is, Rachel needs to believe too.' She boldly met Prince's eyes. 'I mean, she and Prince are unequally yoked.'

He forced his head away. Rebecca was attractive and the low tops she wore was making it hard to concentrate on what she said. He closed his eyes, pretending to pray, but he knew he had to defend his wife. He made himself speak.

'Rachel believes. She's a minister's daughter. She's been a Christian for years.'

The man beside him shook his head. 'Prince, even the demons believe. It takes more. The Bible clearly states that.'

He nodded, but his mind and heart were in turmoil. As the group began their prayers, praying in tongues, sometimes over the top of each other, he found himself surrounded by the group and hands laid on him. Caught up in the atmosphere, he prayed in tongues along with them. He knew without a doubt he was experiencing something supernatural beyond what Rachel ever had. More than anything he wanted her to share this experience— this sign of salvation and filling of the Spirit that left him on such a spiritual high. The prayers of this group had saved his wife and twins when they were on the operating table in the hospital. Perhaps they could now save Rachel's tiredness and her soul … if her soul needed saving.

***

'Rachel?'

She had been dozing on the lounge when Prince arrived home and her eyes opened with a start.

'Prince. You're home. How'd it go?'

He frowned and she couldn't help thinking he looked confused and drained. 'I don't know. It wasn't what I expected. I don't even know for sure what happened but we need to talk.'

Her heart begin to beat faster but she just nodded.

He sat down beside her. 'Do you think you could have depression?'

She stared at him. Where had that come from? She was tired, sure. And a bit more emotional than usual. But she was also getting less sleep and had had major surgery. She was caring for newborn babies!

She was about to say no when she remembered her tears that evening. She had stood looking at Blythe, wishing her own parents could see her, and the tears had started. But Kylie had understood her sadness. She had reassured her it was normal to grieve for lost loved ones and to wish they could see their grandchildren. Even Kylie had shown rare emotion.

'Um, I don't know. Why?'

He reached a hand to her cheek. 'You just seem so tired and sad.'

He looked tired and sad at that moment too. The knowledge brought unbidden tears to her eyes again. Why couldn't she stop them? She wanted to ask him about the prayer meeting, about the people in the church, but all she could do was cry.

He held her close. 'It's okay if you do. Sorry, I didn't want to make you cry.'

She sniffled. 'It's okay. I just need sleep. But I want to hear about tonight. Tell me what happened.'

He closed his eyes tight. 'I wish I could but my head feels all fuzzy. Maybe I'm tired too.'

She chuckled. Maybe he did wake up all through the night when she got up to Blythe. He had offered to bottle feed, but he always seemed so deeply asleep she hated to wake him.

'It was weird, Rach. But kind of amazing.'

Her eyes flew to his. He was rubbing his forehead as though trying to clear his thoughts.

'What happened?'

'They laid hands on me and prayed, and I don't exactly know what happened, but I think I might have blacked out or something. I woke up on the floor. At first I felt like I had to fight for my life, but then I started speaking in tongues—Deborah calls it a heavenly language—and peace came over me and I knew everything was okay.'

Rachel stared at him. This was way out of her experience. Yes, she had heard of tongues before, and supernatural experiences like prophecies and healing. But blacking out? She wasn't sure about that one. What was the purpose in that? What good did it do, especially if Prince came home so drained?

'Rach, I'd love you to experience it too.' He reached for her. 'And it would help them get to know who you really are and that they don't need to worry about you.'

She stared at the sun-tanned hand resting on hers and wondered at the way her heart thundered. It was all a bit too overwhelming right now. Her world felt shaken. She had never spoken in tongues herself, but she knew her ability to write poems and songs was a gift from God. Sometimes the words would flow from somewhere deep; somewhere beyond herself, and she would know God was speaking through her. Was that how it was for Prince when he spoke in tongues?

He took her hand in his. 'Once Seton is allowed home, will you come to church with me?'

There was a pleading quality to his voice and she couldn't say no. She found herself nodding. How could she refuse when he looked at her like that? But it would be harder once Seton was home and there were two babies to care for. 'I'll need your help with the babies.'

He nodded. 'Of course. Deborah and Parker will help too. They want to introduce us all to the church.'

Her heart lurched. She wasn't going to let Deborah touch her twins if she could help it. 'Even though we haven't officially accepted the job yet?'

He nodded. 'I think they believe we will.'

Rachel wasn't convinced.

Chapter Seven

Rachel buttoned her blouse with shaking hands. This was her first outing with the twins and there was so much to remember. Seton had been home for almost a week and he was strong and healthy. But having two babies to care for was a lot different from caring for one.

'Are you nearly ready?' Prince sounded like an excited school boy. She wasn't sure if he was more excited that she was coming to church with him, or if he was excited about showing off the twins. 'Almost.'

He stepped into the room and eyed her clothes. She sensed disapproval. He was wearing his smart new suit and she had to admit he looked impressive, but unfamiliar. He moved to the wardrobe and pulled out a dress. 'Can you wear this one?'

'Prince.' She laughed. 'I've had twins. I'm not that size again yet.'

He had the grace to look ashamed before he came to her and drew her into his arms. 'That's okay. You look beautiful just the way you are.'

She wished she could believe him. She raced to the twins' room where Kylie was changing Seton.

'I don't even know why you're going.' Kylie didn't look up as she spoke. 'You're not ready. You're just making more work for yourself.'

Rachel sighed. 'I'm going because it means so much to Prince.'

Kylie shook her head in disgust. 'If Prince really cared he'd notice how hard it is for you to care for the twins and wouldn't ask this of you. You won't hear a thing anyway. They'll cry all the way through.'

'You could come with me.'

Kylie let out a snort and Rachel knew it wasn't worth pushing. Kylie wasn't a Christian and had never understood her commitment to God. She longed to tear down the barrier that seemed to be between herself and God since she had the children and maybe this was the way to do it. Maybe she would be able to write and sing again.

'Ready?' Prince poked his head in the doorway and she felt like crying. Yes, she was ready but the twins weren't. She needed to take a bottle for them and some nappies and … she couldn't think what else right now.

Then Prince screwed up his nose. 'What's that smell?'

She sighed. 'Blythe's dirty. Give me five minutes.'

He shuffled restlessly and gave a dry laugh. 'We're going to be late, but I can't really ask you bring her smelling like that, can I?'

***

Prince hurried up the church ramp, pushing the babies' pram while Rachel tried to keep up, carrying the nappy bag. A man at the door handed her a church newsletter and something in a small white wrapper. She glanced at the writing on the packet. Mint. She shoved it into the nappy bag and followed Prince through the door. And then the music hit her.

Why did she feel so smothered and afraid? Was it the noise? Smiling people welcomed them and crowded over the twins. She wanted to ask them to back off and let them sleep but found herself just smiling at people and wishing the music wasn't affecting her emotions the way it was.

'Rachel! I'm Rebecca.'

She looked up at the young woman, unable to help staring at the sleeveless top with low cleavage and tight fitted skirt displaying a perfect figure.

Rebecca gave a careful smile. 'We've been praying for your salvation.'

She didn't answer but shock hit her. These people didn't even believe she was a Christian!

'Prince, it's so good to see you managed to bring your wife along!' Rebecca's words were said quietly into Prince's ear as she put an arm around his shoulder. Annoyance built up inside Rachel. Rebecca said the word 'wife' as though it were an insult. Obviously Rebecca didn't think Rachel deserved a husband like Prince. Her whole manner was patronising and demeaning.

Prince had begun heading down the front of the church but Rachel grabbed his arm. 'Prince, can we sit down the back?'

His face fell. 'But they want to introduce us. And if we're down the front they'll be able to …' He looked unsure.

'Able to what?'

He bit his lip. 'You'll be able to enjoy the whole experience. They'll be able to lay hands on you.'

That decided it. There was no way she was sitting down the front and have people who didn't even believe she was a Christian lay hands on her. 'We can't sit there, Prince. The babies.' At his questioning look she explained. 'If they cry, I don't want to have to distract everyone when I take them out.'

He shrugged and found a seat at the back.

The service began and the music built up until both babies screamed. Rachel knew they were not going to get their morning sleep. She tried rocking the pram and glanced to Prince who was giving her a sympathetic look. 'Want me to take them out?' he mouthed.

She shook her head like she always did these days when

he offered to help. She tried to listen, but instead found herself desperate for the life she had had as a teenager when her parents were still alive. She had only to care for herself and her daily times with God had brought such joy. She had prayed constantly for Prince to come to know God. But now things had turned around and maybe Prince was even praying the same for her.

I do know you, don't I, God? Of course she did, so why was there such a feeling of disquiet in her soul?

The children refused to settle and Deborah came to the back of the church and reached out her hands. 'I'll take them.'

Rachel stubbornly shook her head. Then Blythe was sick all down her blouse and she turned to Prince, tears filling her eyes.

'We need to go home.'

Deborah gave her a look of disapproval. 'Didn't you bring a change of clothes?'

She didn't answer. Instead she pushed the pram with the crying babies out of the church and waited for Prince to follow. Silently, he helped her put the pram and children in the car, while she held her head, feeling as though she couldn't stand the crying a moment longer.

It only took a few moments of the car being in motion for the children to fall asleep. Prince glanced in her direction. 'That's better!'

To her own dismay, she burst into tears. She felt the car pull over and heard the engine die, but still she couldn't stop.

Prince's arms came around her. 'Rachel, what's wrong?' His voice was pleading, but she didn't know how to put it into words. Instead she allowed him to pull her close, holding her tight. There was comfort with his arms around her, but her mind was still in turmoil.

'I told you.' Kylie held the door open for them as they unloaded the car and brought the twins inside. Rachel rubbed red eyes, put the twins to bed, then lay down herself.

She was awoken by the sound of voices in the dining room.

Deborah and Parker. What were they doing here? She moved to the door to listen.

'You can't let little things like baby sick send you home.' That was Parker's voice. 'I mean, if that's all it takes for Satan to win, he doesn't have to try very hard.'

'It's Rachel's heart we need to be praying about,' Deborah argued with her husband. 'Let's not lecture Prince. It wasn't his choice to leave.'

Rachel closed her eyes and leaned her head against the door. A gentle knock made her jump. Kylie came in, her eyes understanding.

'Can I kick them out?'

Rachel pictured Kylie doing just that and gave a half smile. 'Better not. They pay our rent and for all this.' She waved her hand at the new furniture around her.

'Yes, but this is your house. You don't have to listen to them spouting all that rubbish.'

Rachel moved back to the bed and sat down. 'But what if they're right?' Her heart beat faster at the mere thought.

Kylie plopped down on the bed. 'Rach, you can't let this get to you. They don't know what they're talking about!' She stopped and they both listened to the voices continuing in the lounge room. Kylie scowled. 'They're unsubtle, they bowl people over and they think they know better than anyone else. Don't you remember your faith? Your poems? Your parents and all they stood for?'

Rachel managed a small smile. 'I never thought you'd be the one encouraging me in my faith.'

Kylie looked sheepish as she stood and went to the bookshelf across the room. 'I found these.' She reached for a folder on the shelf and handed them to her cousin. 'Remember writing these?'

Rachel looked down at the poems and songs, nodding her head. 'I used to be so sure of myself. So sure of my faith!' She fingered the pages. 'But now I just don't know.'

Kylie's mouth dropped open. 'You don't believe anymore?'

'What? Yes, of course I believe! But I wonder if I'm pleasing God. I have doubts about whether I'm fully living for God the way he wants me to. Prince keeps talking about living a life filled with the spirit and all this supernatural stuff happens to him now at those meetings. Even the Bible talks about tongues and prophecies and spiritual gifts like that. Am I missing something?'

Her confession brought an ache to her heart so strong it physically hurt. Confusion was sending her world into a darkness that frightened her.

'Rachel, stop it.' Kylie grabbed the folder from Rachel's hands and flipped through until she stopped at a poem. She nimbly slid it out and handed it to her cousin.

'Read this. Talk to God.'

With that, she left the room. Rachel glanced at the poem she had written, remembering it well. A tight lump grew in her throat.

The Lord will restore a song of joy
to your heart which silent falls,
He will bind the wounds, heal the hurts
while you're too tired to call.

He listens as a brother while
you cannot bare your heart,
He hears the cries you can't express—
which leave you torn apart.

He'll lift you up on eagles' wings
as you wait upon His name,
I pray today He'll touch your life
and take away your pain!

I know He's walking by your side—
your comfort, strength and friend,

He'll bring you through this shadowed time,
and your sun will shine again.

Chapter Eight

Tori fingered the corner of her free 'stolen' blanket, wishing its warmth would fill the coldness of her heart. Kenny had been angry with her for grabbing a blanket that wasn't meant to be hers. She had inadvertently taken one he said was meant for him.

'You could have ruined everything,' he hissed at her, shaking it in her face.

'How?' She asked the question in a dull, flat voice but her interest was piqued.

He opened a corner of the blanket and pointed to a pocket stitched inside. 'Your future. My future. It all depends on this. You grabbed the blanket meant for me. They might stop coming if it gets too risky, and we're almost rich, Aura. They've promised us a mansion. I only have to prove myself on two more jobs and we'll be done.'

He took out a little plastic wrapped package. Mints. They weren't going to fill anybody up. Then realisation hit her. They weren't mints. They were drugs. They came through the blankets. Dealers traded drugs that way. Who would have guessed? She almost laughed. A church was dealing drugs. Ingenious.

She pulled her blanket up around her shoulders. She'd settled well into the homeless life, but there had been too many arrests lately. She couldn't afford to be arrested. Once her identity was discovered she would never see freedom again. Kenny's promised mansion sounded good but it wasn't worth the risk of being caught. He promised them he could buy them anything they wanted in a few weeks. But what did she want? She didn't know.

She drew in a deep breath, feeling the pain where Trojan had struck her that morning. It probably wasn't on purpose, but drug-fuelled rages had no purpose. Tension was building the more wealth Kenny promised.

Tori sighed, drawing the blanket closer. Her fingers stopped on a lump in the corner. She looked closer, reading the words embroidered on the hem line. 'Happy Kingdom Church'. Life. She wished she knew what it was all about.

That man named Prince who let her get away with the blanket probably had a perfect life. She had seen something in his eyes that shone like the stars that twinkled above her at night. He didn't look like the type to deal drugs. But even her blanket had a 'mint' hidden inside it.

In that moment, she knew she needed to leave. She didn't say a word, she didn't have a plan, she just began walking down the road, away from Kenny and the gang.

***

Prince went to answer the phone, his heart sinking. If it was Deborah asking to visit again, he didn't know what he'd do. He felt torn between his wife and his church. It was an awkward place to be. He took a deep breath and answered.

'What took you so long?' a gruff voice asked.

Prince let out a cry of delight. 'Storm! How are you? Your little niece and nephew have been crying for their uncle day and night!'

'Hmmph. So they're both home. I imagine your life is utter chaos now?'

Prince laughed but it caught in his throat. 'You could say that.' He tried to keep his voice steady but knew he failed.

'I'm coming to stay for a while.'

Prince's mouth dropped open in shock. The voice was Storm's but he couldn't quite believe the words. 'You … what? Why?'

'I'm sick of the roads, that's why. I've got holiday leave.'

'But Storm, the babies cry day and night.'

'Yeah, you told me that. Obviously they need their uncle.'

Prince's eyes widened. Was Storm coming because he thought he could help? No, it couldn't be true. Storm never cared about anyone but himself. But then, he had come to the hospital to see Rachel …

'Have you got a room for me? I'm leaving Dusty Lane at the boarding stables and I can't be bothered bringing my caravan.'

Prince cleared his throat. 'Um, yeah sure, but I'd better check with Rachel first.'

'Why?' Storm's question sounded like an accusation. 'Have you got a room or not?'

'We have a room, but—'

'Good. I'm coming.'

Prince let the phone fall into his lap. What next? How was he going to tell Rachel Storm had decided to come and stay? And what would Deborah and Parker think? They had told him he needed to rid his house of all ungodliness. Storm had defied God and mocked him his whole life.

***

Tori hitchhiked some of the distance she was travelling and walked the rest of the time. She trudged along a partially built highway, glad to have a road to follow with no traffic to contend with. The workers had gone home for the day, but surely someone had left something she might be able to eat? She was tired and hungry.

Then she saw it. A caravan all by itself a little way from the road. With eyes of hope she quietly made her way toward it.

All seemed quiet. She knocked on the door, then escaped

around the side. No response. Quickly, she began work on the door. She needed to get inside.

The first thing she saw on the table was holiday approval for Storm Clements.

'Good! I have at least two weeks.' She folded the piece of paper and started as her stomach gave a fierce rumble. The kitchen area was small, but the fridge was on. She opened it and to her delight found fresh fruit inside. She closed the door and allowed her eyes to roam the tins of food along a shelf above the small stove. Then she opened a cupboard door and smiled. Storm Clements kept himself well stocked and she planned to make use of it.

Where would she find a can opener? Her mother always kept one in the second drawer. She pulled it open and scrabbled through the contents. Bingo! She could feast for two weeks! Or could she?

It was strange that the fridge still had fresh fruit. If Storm was really going to be away for two weeks, surely he would have used up his perishables?

What if Storm Clements wasn't really the owner of this van? What if it was someone else who would be back tomorrow? She had to find out somehow … but not until she had some food.

Tori longed to eat and eat but knew it would upset her stomach, which was now so used to being empty. She controlled herself and searched the van. Piles of paper were everywhere. Storm Clements was clearly not a tidy person.

Finally, she found the assurance she wanted. There was a copy of Storm's resume and a photo. This had to be Storm's caravan.

With interest, she began reading. Storm had worked in a circus most of his life, riding horses. He had left school at sixteen and was now working on the roads.

She studied the photo of the young teenager with the unruly mop of hair.

I could make myself look like him. A plan began to form. Storm's dark, messy hair wouldn't take much to imitate. And working in the circus would be an excellent hiding place.

Carefully, Tori took the resume and the photo. She would stay there for two weeks, and then her new life in the circus would begin as 'Storm Clements'. Victoria Seeth lived no more.

***

Storm knocked on the doorstep of the large house, already hearing a baby crying. It was a tiny, plaintive cry that demanded response. He knocked again, and the door opened.

'Storm!' Prince's eyes lit with amusement and something akin to relief.

Storm gave a sheepish grin, then tried to change it to a fierce look. 'You need a shave,' he told his brother. 'Your bristles don't match your fancy new clothes.'

Prince laughed as he pulled Storm into a hug. 'You're right. Not much time to look after myself these days. Reminds me of someone else not so many years ago.'

Storm pretended ignorance but he knew exactly what Prince meant. Young Storm Clements had been known for his mop of wild, curly hair and haphazard ways. Only the constant annoyance of it blowing into his eyes while working on the roads had convinced him to get it cut into a short, neat style. 'So what's with the fancy clothes?'

Prince looked sheepish. 'I've got a new job.'

Storm snorted. 'So you took up that fancy acting job with the church, hey?' He then looked over Prince's shoulder to where Rachel walked down the hallway toward them.

'What's all the commotion?' She glanced down to the swag at Storm's feet, then back to him.

'Storm's come to stay and help out.' Prince's hesitant look told Storm Rachel hadn't been expecting him. 'Been worried about you,' he said in an accusing voice as though she should never dare cause him any concern.

66

To his relief, Rachel's face lit into a brilliant smile. 'Thanks, God!'

Storm screwed up his nose. 'I'm not God. I'm Storm and no, God didn't tell me to come either. I just decided all on my own.'

Rachel's mouth tilted into a smile. 'We'll see.'

Storm rolled his eyes, but couldn't help feeling amused. Rachel was likeable despite her crazy beliefs about God. He kicked at the swag at his feet. 'So where do I fit?'

Prince grinned. 'Let's put him in the room with the babies.'

A look passed over Rachel's face. 'Even you wouldn't want to sleep there, Prince. Why would we do it to your brother?'

Storm didn't miss the hurt in Prince's eyes and wondered at the tension he sensed. What was going on? He had thought Prince and Rachel were the perfect married couple who shared their belief in God and happily ever afters.

Suddenly he swung one arm up around Prince's shoulder and the other around Rachel's. 'So come on, invite me in and show me what to do with the two little terrors.'

***

Prince tried to hide his amusement. Storm was staring at the two little babies, his nose screwed up. It was obvious he'd had nothing to do with babies before.

'Here.' He placed Seton in his brother's arms, and Storm instantly became tense, as though he might break the baby.

'They're still little,' was all he said. Prince laughed. 'You mean they're not cute and responsive yet.'

Storm frowned. 'Something like that. When will they crawl?'

'Not for months. First, they need to develop the strength to hold their own heads up and roll over. Blythe is doing that now, but Seton might take longer.'

Storm just nodded, handing Seton back to Prince. Then he looked his brother in the eye. 'I never thought I'd see you like this, Prince. Looking after your babies and wife and all and being a committed family man. Believing in God sure made a difference to you.'

Prince just nodded, remaining silent. Storm obviously didn't realise just how much time he spent away from home these days. The job was becoming more intense and demanding more of his time. The good news was, if he were to accept the position after the trial was over, his pay would increase and his hours would be less. He just needed to hold out a little bit longer.

Chapter Nine

'I just don't know how you do it!' A sleepy Storm came to the breakfast table with a fierce frown. 'How do you survive on so little sleep?'

Prince looked up from his toast, surprised. 'I sleep.'

Rachel and Kylie gave each other a look, then turned to Storm.

'Some of us are too tired to stay awake while others of us are too tired to sleep,' Kylie said, 'and some of us know we need to respond to the babies, so we can't afford the luxury of sleeping through their cries.'

Prince looked to Rachel. 'The babies were awake through the night?'

'Often!' Storm put in before Rachel could answer.

Prince said nothing but guilt consumed him. He had been determined to help Rachel with these children, not leave her to do all the work on her own. But Rachel seemed so intent on doing it. Did she think he was incompetent, or was she just giving him a break after his many hours of uni and work?

'Rach, how about you go to the Bible study at church tonight, while I look after the twins?'

Uncertainty filled her brown eyes before she slowly shook her head. 'I don't think they want me, Prince. I'm just an added extra they have to include because you married me.'

Was that true? He hoped not but he couldn't deny the

possibility. 'They just need to get to know you. The real you. Why don't you bring along one of your songs? I'll ask if you can sing it for them. I've told them about your gift.'

To his dismay, her eyes filled with tears. 'I don't know why, but I can't sing anymore. Maybe one day I will again, but not yet.'

Kylie had been watching the exchange and glared at him. What had he done now? She was so protective of Rachel. She was giving him a challenging look.

'Why don't you both go out somewhere together? Not to church, but somewhere romantic. I'll look after the twins.'

He looked at Rachel. It would be hard to tell Parker and Deborah he was going out with his wife. They wouldn't understand and would give him that look that made him feel like he'd failed and disappointed God. But for Rachel it was worth it.

She was studying him, looking thoughtful. 'How about I come to the Bible study with you? You keep saying I need to see what they believe and see what I think. I'll feel more confident if you're with me.'

Relief filled him. Then Deborah and Parker might get off his back about Rachel. They would see that she *was* a committed Christian, living a life for God. He smiled his delight. 'That would be great.'

***

Rachel headed to the bedroom to change. Why had she said she would go to the Bible study? Kylie and Storm were bathing the twins, preparing them for bed. She could hear Prince cleaning his teeth in the bathroom and moved to the mirror.

She had never considered herself attractive, even though Prince seemed to think she was. Her eyes were too small and brown. But now her blonde hair was no longer long and shiny as it had been as she was growing up. It was thin and short. The stress of having the twins had caused some of it to fall out. Her eyes were tired, with deep shadows beneath them. She doubted Deborah and Parker really wanted her to be the face of their church. She could understand why they wanted Prince and the twins, but she was too plain. She wasn't fit to be a media star.

'Ready?' Prince came out of the bathroom dressed in his new finery, looking like a movie star. She had to admit he looked good. Too good if Rebecca was going to be there.

She was. She sidled up to Prince the moment they arrived, not even giving Rachel a glance. Her eyes were shining and her low top revealed almost everything.

'God has given me a word for you tonight,' she said. 'Come and have a seat.'

Prince leaned to whisper in Rachel's ear. 'Rebecca's leading tonight.' Then he sat beside Rebecca who crossed her slender legs in her short skirt and smiled around at the group before passing around some mints. Prince unwrapped his and popped it in his mouth whilst Rachel just fiddled with hers, glad to have something to do with her hands.

For what she had expected to be a Bible study, the Bible didn't seem to play a part. Instead, Rebecca gave a prophecy she said God had given her. She spoke of a dragon attempting to steal one of them away with false words and a lying tongue. She began to pray against the dragon, her voice becoming louder and more aggressive as she spoke.

'This dragon which comes disguised as a helpless child will take the blessings from your home.' she began to speak to an imaginary person in the room. 'You will attempt to give of your time, your finances, your gifts, but it will be snatched from you.' Then she turned suddenly to Prince and laid her hands on him.

'You have healed others, now accept healing!' she screeched and the group began to pray all at once.

Rachel stared as Prince fell down and a string of foreign words flowed from his mouth. She began to shake with something akin to fear.

'This is what healed you, Rachel,' a woman suddenly said in Rachel's ear. 'Prince's faith, Prince's gift of healing which came once he was filled with the Holy Spirit.'

Then suddenly Deborah was there by Rachel's side, too close for comfort.

'It's true!' she insisted, as if sensing Rachel's doubt. 'Prince has a gift of healing.'

'And tongues came with that?' Rachel whispered.

'Tongues are the sign.'

'What sign?'

'The sign of his salvation.'

Rachel said nothing, but confusion and turmoil filled her in a way it never had before.

'I see your struggle,' the woman said. 'God has given me that discernment. But Rachel, this struggle is to bring you closer to God. To show you what you need so that you also can be his.'

'I am his,' Rachel responded, frustrated that her voice lacked conviction.

'Come to him, Rachel,' Deborah pleaded. 'Don't work against God, or he will work against you and your family.'

At her words, Rachel found herself breaking down into convulsive sobs. Overwhelmed by it all, she couldn't think.

'God help me!' she cried, and the group all turned to her and began to pray again.

'Praise God for repentance!' one woman screamed out. 'Slay the dragon! Banish it from their home.'

Rachel felt terror. Did these people think she was possessed or something? And why were they screaming at God, demanding things of him? They sounded like children having a tantrum and demanding things of their parents. She couldn't explain it with reason, but she knew in her heart this wasn't right.

'Lord, help me show Prince. Let him see the truth.' Her

words were whispered amidst the turmoil around her and slowly peace stole over her. She sat still, though the noise continued. It was as though there were a refuge around her, a realm of peace that these people couldn't destroy.

By the time they headed home, Rachel was desperate to see the children again. She didn't speak, and neither did Prince. He seemed drained now, the way he always was when he returned from the meetings. No wonder! No one could expend that kind of energy without feeling drained afterwards. Her mind swam. Had they unwittingly become involved in a cult? Who could she ask?

Prince broke the silence. 'I prayed and prayed for what happened tonight.'

She stared into his handsome profile. 'What was that?'

'You know ...'

'I don't know,' Rachel confessed. 'I don't know anything anymore. But I don't want to go back there. Those people are manipulating and forceful. I can't think with them screaming in my face.'

Prince looked horrified. 'Rachel, those people are the reason you and the twins are alive today!'

Rachel sat up straight. 'No Prince, God is the reason!' Anger built up within her 'What makes you think those people have special favours with him?'

He fell quiet a moment, then admitted. 'Because they told me.'

Rachel laughed scornfully and neither said another word the rest of the trip home. But she saw the way he held his head as though he had a painful headache. She had hurt and disappointed him. Guilt consumed her but she couldn't bring herself to apologise. Right now her anger was stronger than her guilt.

Chapter Ten

Storm pushed the mower back and forth across the yard. He gritted his teeth, taking out his frustration on the long grass. He hated the tension he felt in this home. So much needed doing, but Prince was always out somewhere with something important to do. It was as though he thought it was Storm's job to keep up with the everyday workload. He didn't mind helping out a bit, but Prince should be doing his bit too.

He looked up to see his brother step out the door, dressed in all his finery, giving him a quick wave. Enough was enough. He stopped the mower. 'Hey, wait! Where are you going this time?'

Prince unlocked the car and opened the door without really looking at Storm. 'A church meeting.'

'Dressed like a business guru?'

Prince grinned. 'Come on, you know I look good.'

'You look stupid. You look like you're trying to be someone you're not.'

Prince's grin faded. 'I need to honour God with my whole life, Storm. That includes the way I dress. It's a witness to others.'

'A witness of what? Your pride? Your wealth?'

Prince frowned. 'Storm, I'm going. You can let fly with your opinions later.'

'Does Rachel know?'

'Know what?'

'Where you're going?'

Prince didn't answer. Storm felt familiar fury rise up within him and pushed it down. He wasn't a hot-headed child any longer. He needed to be rational and talk this through. He made his way toward his brother. 'Well, does she?'

Prince avoided his eyes. 'She knows I'm going to work.'

'And she's happy for you to go?'

'Not exactly, but we're working it out.'

Storm stared into his brother's handsome face. 'I don't get you.'

Prince hesitated. 'What's there to get?'

'Why you leave here every chance you get. You're hardly home these days. You have an amazing wife, two children … noisy, often crying children yes, but two children just the same. What's your issue? I thought your religion changed you and you had stopped running from responsibility.'

Prince dropped the car keys and they fell to the ground with a clunk. He didn't even look at them. 'You think I'm running?'

'Yes.'

'From Rachel?'

'Yes.'

Prince shook his head and bent to pick up the keys. 'I'm not running from Rachel. I provide well for them, Storm. And I have learned to put God and his will before my own desires. I have to do what God has asked of me. I owe it to him.'

'Says who?'

'God.'

'What, his big voice boomed from the sky and told you that?'

'No, he gave … never mind.'

Storm couldn't believe what he was hearing. Impulsively, he stepped on the keys and kicked them out of Prince's reach. Then he grabbed his brother by the shirt and shoved him against the car.

'How dare you! You seduce the most decent girl there is, get her pregnant, marry her, then treat her as though she doesn't even exist. All in the name of God. I bet God is planning to strike you down with lightning for even thinking of linking his name with your misguided ideas.'

Prince froze, his expression shocked. Storm released his shirt front, then stepped back. Prince's hand went to his chest and straightened the creases. 'Look Storm, I know you won't understand, but I was given some words of knowledge.'

'Huh?' Storm wished he understood the jargon of Prince's beliefs.

'God gave some people some words to tell me. They said God wants me to prove my love for him—to put aside my family and show my dedication to him. They saw a vision …' His voice trailed off and Storm knew his scepticism was written clearly on his face.

'What vision?'

'When I was in hospital praying that Rachel would live. They saw me trying to cling to Rachel and the twins but it was smothering them. It was only when I let go that they started to breathe again.'

'Who told you that?'

'Deborah and Parker. Deborah saw the vision and knew God wanted her to tell me.'

'So why didn't God tell you himself?'

Prince shrugged. 'I don't know. I don't get visions and things. It's not my gift.'

'But why would God tell you to let go of the people he's put right under your nose who desperately need you? Doesn't sound like a loving God to me. Doesn't sound like the God Rachel believes in, or the God I thought you believed in.'

A perplexed expression crossed Prince's face before he bit his lip. 'Look, I haven't abandoned them. I'm just learning to trust God more with them. I'm trying to find the balance between work and family. It's been a rough time, Storm. I've got a lot to sort out.'

Storm bent to pick up the car keys. 'If you had any sense

in your head you'd work it out right here with Rachel. All that stuff you just spouted at me is absolute—' He cut himself off, tempering his words. 'It's garbage.' He threw the keys at Prince.

Prince caught the keys against his chest and shook his head with a sigh. 'Don't give me that disgusted look, Storm. You've thrown it around your whole life and it means nothing to me now. I'm glad you're here helping, I really am … but I've got to go.'

With that, he got into the car, slid the keys into the ignition, gave Storm one last troubled look and drove away. Storm's final memory was of the baby car seats sitting empty in the back of the vehicle.

He headed inside, wondering what to tell Rachel. Maybe he should just go back to his caravan out on the roads. He hated drama, so what was he doing here?

***

Rachel set the table, leaving one place empty.

'Where's Prince?' Kylie nodded her head toward his empty place.

'Another church meeting.'

'Are you sure?'

Rachel's brows raised. 'You think he went somewhere else?'

Kylie shrugged. 'I don't know. He just has a lot of Bible studies and things he goes to. And you told me about that Rebecca lady. I just can't see her not taking advantage of the fact that she's single and available and you're stuck here at home with the children.'

Rachel's heart sank. Even Kylie could see something had changed. Prince always came back from his meetings on edge or completely drained. Something was different about him. She sank into Prince's chair, and let her head fall into her hands.

'I think you can trust him, Rachel.'

Her eyes darted to where Storm now stood in the doorway. 'I know he's not acting himself, but he's been through a lot. I mean, with you being so sick when you had the twins and

77

everything. I think he was really scared. You know that Mum died having Beauty and I?'

Tears sprang to Rachel's eyes and she tried to hold them back, knowing Storm never had time for tears. To her surprise he came and gave her an awkward pat on the shoulder.

'Rachel, the day he married you … well, even I couldn't believe how serious he was about you. I mean, for the first time in his life I could see he actually loved a girl.'

'Loved …' Rachel began.

Storm shook his head, then jumped up. 'Where's your wedding photos?'

Rachel pointed to an album in the bookshelf against the wall. He pulled the album down from the shelf and shoved it into her lap. 'You need to sit here and look at these for a while.'

As he flipped open the album, Rachel felt like a child getting into trouble. Storm's manner was officious; that was, until he sat down beside her and turned the page.

She stared at the picture of herself dressed in her beautiful white wedding gown.

'I wore white,' she muttered as memories began to stir in her heart. She was pregnant but wearing a white wedding gown. She had always thought it was tradition not to if you weren't a virgin, but Prince had insisted she was forgiven and pure before God. And that was the way Prince had seen her.

'You look pretty happy if you ask me,' Storm said quietly.

Kylie smiled at the photo. 'You gave me a copy of that one. It was your favourite.'

Storm went through the photos, giving a running narrative. Rachel found her memories recaptured as she stared at the photos of herself and Prince. She couldn't have asked for a better-looking husband. His dark, intense eyes and expressive face still had her heart beating fast every time she looked at it. And yes, even she had looked beautiful that day. A fierce protectiveness overwhelmed her. God had given her Prince. She would not let him go without a fight!

'You'll sort it out,' Storm assured her. 'When Prince is being confusing, when he doesn't seem to be paying attention, just look back to your wedding day and remember his love for you. That sort of love never dies.'

Rachel smiled. 'That's what I do when God's being confusing too.'

Storm gave her a quizzical look and she shrugged. 'When I don't understand what God's doing and he doesn't seem to be listening, I look back to when he died because he loved me so much. That kind of love never dies.'

Storm bit his lip, as though holding back the negative things he wanted to say. Finally, he shrugged. 'Whatever floats your boat.'

***

Rachel smiled as she waited for Prince to return and remembered Storm's off-hand response. As much as he tried to convince the world he was cold and hard, every now and then he slipped and blew his cover.

Her smile faded as a car came in the drive and her heart skipped a beat. She glanced out the window.

Prince was home.

She had to believe he loved her and make an effort. She moved toward him as the door opened, but he didn't notice her. He walked straight down the hall into the twins' room. Hesitating just a moment, she raced after him and found him looking down into Seton's cot.

She cleared her throat and forced herself to be cheerful. 'Welcome home.' It sounded stiff and formal but she was trying.

He glanced up with a brief smile before running a finger across Seton's cheek. 'Thanks.'

He moved to Blythe's cot.

'How was the meeting?'

He shrugged broad shoulders beneath his smart shirt. 'It didn't go quite the way I expected.'

She studied him. 'In what way?'

He sat down in the feeding chair in the room and sighed. 'Rach, I understand that you can't take the job. I understand that you can't be involved in the media presentation of the church. I told Parker I need to resign.'

Resign? Relief filled her and she moved to rest a hand on his shoulder. 'I think you've done the right thing, even though it will make it harder for us financially.' She tilted her head. 'But how do you feel about giving up your dream?'

His mouth tightened. 'Well, they gave me another option.' He hesitated, then took a deep breath. 'They said we can use an actor instead of you.'

An actor. And have Prince and the twins in photos with another woman? Wasn't the point of having their family meant to be that they would be a real family supporting the beliefs and ideals of the church? Maybe Prince was beginning to, but she simply couldn't.

Prince was fiddling with his shirt cuff. 'The actor they suggested is Rebecca.'

Rachel couldn't help her gasp.

He hurried on. 'It wouldn't mean anything.'

Anger built up within her. How dare they? She could see what was happening, even if he couldn't.

His dark eyes questioned her. 'You don't like Rebecca?'

'She doesn't like *me*. And even if you can't see it, she likes you a little bit too much.'

Hurt filled his eyes but his naivety made her angrier. She spelled it out for him. 'They don't want you to act, Prince. They want you to divorce me and marry her!'

Prince laughed, but it was hollow. 'What?'

'They've been grooming you for their purposes all along. They're a cult. They're going to convince you to marry Rebecca.'

'Don't you even trust me?' His eyes now blazed with anger. 'I resist all temptation, I avert my eyes when an attractive woman flirts with me, and you still don't trust me?'

Her heart dropped. 'You find Rebecca attractive?'

Prince left the room without another word. She watched him go, then heard Seton begin to cry, closely followed by Blythe.

She rubbed her hands across her eyes, squeezing them shut. So much for making an effort.

***

Prince stalked out the back door. He didn't know what to do. He had never seen Rachel so angry with him. He had to admit the idea of working with Rebecca made him uncomfortable, but surely Rachel could have discussed it with him reasonably? She didn't have to throw accusations at him and insinuate he had no morals. It hurt. Deeply.

'Oh, so you thought you'd come back home, did you?' Storm's deep voice startled him and he jumped.

Storm chuckled. 'Uptight, aren't we?'

Prince glared at his brother. He was pruning a bush Prince had planned to prune a long time ago, before the Happy Kingdom Church had taken so much of his time.

'Yes, I am.' He hadn't meant to snap.

Storm's brows rose. 'So what's got you worked up? Finally worked out you should never have left your wife for that church.'

Prince grit his teeth. 'I have not left my wife for the church, so get off my back.'

Storm studied him for a moment, then sat down on the brick ledge nearby. He patted the spot beside him. Prince hesitated before sitting.

'So what's happened?'

Prince would never have imagined telling Storm, but he needed to vent and Storm was there.

'Rachel's not keen to be a church media representative and they want a whole family, so they want to bring in someone else.'

Storm nodded. 'Makes sense to me. So what's the problem?'

'Rachel's not happy about it. They want to still use the twins and I but bring in an actor.'

Storm quirked a brow. 'What, and try to fool the public that you and this strange woman are a happily married family?'

'She's not a strange woman. It's Rebecca from church. And it's not fooling or deceiving. It's called acting.'

Storm leaned back, putting on his most sarcastic voice. 'Ah, now I get it. So it's okay because it's acting, even though the public will think it's real, or are supposed to think it's real. And I suppose they'll realise that being a part of this church will bring your family closer together like it has done for yours.'

'Storm, if we're paid to do it, it's acting.'

Storm stood. 'Okay. So how about you pay me to act as Rachel's husband while you go off with this other woman you're paid to be with? The world can think I'm Rachel's real husband. After all, I'm here more than you are.' He narrowed his eyes, glaring. 'I'd do it, you know, but the funny thing is, Rachel is in love with you so even if I tried to seduce her she wouldn't do it. Unlike you.'

Prince couldn't believe his ears. Storm had gone too far! Anger surged up inside and exploded as he grabbed Storm by his collar and shoved him backwards. He lost his balance and fell onto the ground, but within a few seconds he was up, his furious face centimetres from Prince's, shoving him back.

Prince clenched his fist. 'Back off, Storm. I'm trying to control myself here, so don't push. I'd have punched you in the face by now, but Rachel protected it at her cost back in high school, so I won't do it for her sake.'

Storm's jaw jumped. 'You forget I'm bigger now too,

brother. And the only reason I won't smash *your* pretty face right now is that Rachel loves it. Though I don't know why because you don't deserve her!'

Prince drew in a deep breath. What if Rachel had seen what has just happened? She didn't need more distress.

Lord, help me. What am I doing? He took a deep breath.

'Storm, I think you'd better leave.'

Storm glared at him a moment before nodding and heading into the house. Prince knew he would be packing. Rachel would want to know why. What could he say?

God, where are you? I need your help. Show me what to do about the job. It seemed to be your provision but I never thought it would cost me my relationship with my family. Show me what to do.

Chapter Eleven

Tori searched the caravan one last time. Time was up. Storm Clements was due back any day, but at least she had a job to go to, if only she could find a circus. With hope filling her, she took Storm's passport photo, his resume and his birth certificate.

The road seemed empty as she came from her hiding place and studied the scenery around her. It would only take a few hours before the traffic began on the highway nearby, and she wanted to be off this new road before the workmen arrived. She also wanted to get a ride from a truckie, rather than someone whose occupation was a mystery. It seemed safer to know something about the person you were hitchhiking with and she knew a little about truckies. Sarah's father was one. Despite Mick's one fight with her mother which caused him to leave, he'd never been a violent man and Tori had trusted him.

The first truck to slow was an empty cattle truck. Her heart hammered as it hissed to a stop. Was she crazy to accept a ride from a stranger? Self-defence was useless if the driver was dangerous. She hated the helpless feeling she had so often felt at the hands of her mother and the anger it had left behind, but she also knew it was wiser not to fight back.

She screwed up her nose at the remnant of the cattle's smell wafted up to greet her and focussed on the cabin door. She needed a lift and if she was killed, what had she lost anyway? Her life, but what was that worth? Taking a deep breath, she watched as the driver opened his window and leaned out, yelling above the roar of the motor. 'Need a lift?'

She nodded.

'Good, because I need some company to keep me awake.' He threw his thumb toward the passenger door, indicating she should get in.

Heaving herself high up into the cabin, she wondered if she'd made the right choice. He wanted someone to keep him awake, she wanted to withdraw into her own silent world. But she owed him.

He put the truck into gear and roared off before glancing at her then back to the road. 'You seem a bit young to be out on your own.'

She shrugged. 'I'm not on my own. I have a job waiting for me in the circus.'

His brow rose. 'Your family know about it?'

Her mind worked fast. 'My grandma brought me up. She's all I've got but she's got dementia now.'

He threw her a look of sympathy. 'Want to talk about it?'

'No.' One lie was not enough. She needed another one to distract him. Something that she could talk about for a long time. Something close to the truth but far enough from it to mislead him. She glanced at his face. He reminded her of Sarah's dad. 'My best friend's dad is a truckie.'

It worked. She talked about Sarah's dad and shared the stories he'd told her. The driver shared his own and the common ground kept them going until they reached a town and Tori asked to be dropped off.

The first thing she did was find a hairdresser. The young hairdresser appeared to have no qualms about cutting her hair. The girl didn't even try to hide her disgust and screwed up her nose as she shampooed the dirty, bedraggled locks. She chewed on her gum, looking bored and waiting for her instructions.

Tori sighed. What had she become? Her mother would be aghast to see her beautiful daughter sitting in front of a half-hearted, amateur hairdresser, having her hair darkened and shaped into a mop of curls.

But her mother didn't even deserve a thought.

'That what you're after?' The girl stopped chewing her gum long enough to ask the question, then looked at Tori in the mirror, head to one side.

Tori stared at the hair she could hardly recognise. 'Perfect. Can I use your toilets before I go?'

The girl nodded and pointed down the back of the shop. Tori breathed a sigh of relief. This was her only way out. She had no money to pay the girl and needed to escape without being followed. She walked out the back door, discreetly pocketing a bottle of tanning powder from the shelf as she went. Once out the back door she headed out onto the street and then moved quickly, messing up her hair into the haphazard style of young Storm Clements in her photo. She brushed some of the tanning powder onto her face as she walked, darkening her pale skin. Many years of modelling had made her a pro at putting on make-up on the run and her nimble fingers worked efficiently.

Next stop—local shops. She needed boy's clothes. Clothes like Storm would wear. But as she wandered through the local Big W, she knew she wouldn't get away with new clothes. She needed to steal second-hand clothes from somewhere. The Salvation Army or St Vincent's would have to do. As she thought on it, she wished she had been through Storm's wardrobe in the caravan and taken something from there.

It felt strange stealing from a Salvation Army store. For years her mother had dressed her in the latest styles with the most expensive clothes she could buy, and now she was looking like a reckless, unwashed, boy. She studied herself in a shop window and almost smiled at the sight. Tori Seeth existed no more.

***

Storm didn't go straight back to his caravan on the roads. Prince and Rachel clearly needed help, more help than he knew how to give. Their belief in God didn't make sense, but it had made them happy. Normally, he didn't care about anybody's happiness, not even his own. He didn't understand why he was doing this, but he needed to see his eldest brother, Blaze.

Blaze worked as a youth pastor in a church and Storm knew his faith was unshakeable. He had questioned and mocked Blaze's faith often but never succeeded in convincing him to give it up.

Faith in God was the only thing he could think of that would help Prince and Rachel. They had been so content before, but now Prince was being a blind idiot. Storm felt no need for faith himself, but his brother and sister-in-law needed it desperately.

He rolled his eyes at the cry of joy his brother gave as he opened the door. 'Bonnie! Sky! You'll never guess who's here!'

Storm grunted as he was engulfed in a big hug, then tolerated the same from Blaze's wife, and the little dark haired girl who had raced to the door from another room.

Storm couldn't help smiling down at Sky. Prince's first daughter, now four years old. She bounced around his knees, excited to see him and trying to hug his leg. Blaze and Bonnie fostered her and he knew Prince had planned to take her back one day. Would that happen now? What would happen if Prince and Rachel didn't sort out their issues? They had to. For Sky's sake. For everyone's sake.

'Come in, sit down.' Blaze urged him forward with a hand to his back as though afraid he would run away.

Storm shook his hand off. 'Okay, okay. I'm coming.' He plopped himself onto the lounge, shoving aside the Bible that sat on the cushion. Honestly, these people were fanatical about their religion!

Blaze reached forward and moved it onto the coffee table,

87

his smile still in place. 'So how are you?'

Storm frowned. 'I'm not here about me. I'm here about your other brother and his wife.' He saw the way Bonnie bit her lip as though holding back a smile. He didn't understand why so many in his family seemed to find his gruff manner amusing. Most people in the world were offended by it and he was more comfortable with that.

Blaze leaned forward in his chair. 'Okay. So how are Prince and Rachel?'

He glanced to the little girl still gazing at him like he was some kind of hero. Sky was too young to take any notice of his words, but still he was cautious. 'Physically, they're well.'

Blaze and Bonnie seemed to let out a collective sigh of relief. The meow of a cat in the next room distracted Sky and she ran off after it. Good. Now he didn't have to measure his every word. He glared at Blaze and Bonnie. 'If you're so concerned, why haven't you been to see them?'

Blaze's brow shot to his hairline. 'I've been desperate to see them, but when I asked about coming Prince said Rachel wasn't ready for visitors. I didn't like to push.'

'I didn't ask. I just turned up on their doorstep.'

Blaze chuckled. 'Why doesn't that surprise me? How'd they take it?'

Storm sat up straighter. 'They were pretty happy to see me. But ...'

Blaze seemed to pick up on Storm's hesitation. 'But what?'

He saw the glance that passed between Blaze and Bonnie before Bonnie came to sit directly beside him. He made himself sit still and not move away as he wanted to. She put a hand on his arm. 'What's going on, Storm?'

He looked pointedly at her hand and she wisely removed it. She should know by now that he was not the touchy feely type. He shrugged. 'I think you need to see them.'

Blaze frowned. 'They asked us not to. I want to respect that.'

Storm gave them his best disgusted look. 'Fine. Respect it then.' He stood. 'Looks like there's nothing more for me to do here.'

He turned to leave but Blaze grabbed his arm and spun him back around. 'Tell me what's going on, Storm.'

Storm narrowed his eyes, softening when he saw the genuine love and concern in Blaze's expression. 'Their marriage is dying. Prince has got a weird new religion and forgotten his real faith.' He didn't know how else to put it. Thankfully Sky was busy playing on the floor and didn't seem to be listening.

Blaze stepped back as though he'd been struck. He opened and closed his mouth a few times before Bonnie stepped forward.

'I thought you didn't believe.' Her eyes held a hope he felt cruel to squash, but he had to.

'I don't.' He shrugged. 'But believing gave them … well, it changed Prince, didn't it? He was so everywhere. He had no real purpose or morals or anything. And Rachel was pretty special and I think it was because of what she believed. I dunno, I just couldn't help respecting her or something.' Storm sighed. 'I'm not making any sense, am I?'

Blaze didn't answer, but his eyes took on a look of understanding. He threw his arms around his brother, gave him a fierce hug, then stepped back. 'Thank you, Storm. Invite or no invite, Bonnie and I will head down to see them as soon as I can organise leave with the church and find someone to look after Sky.' He went to ruffle Storm's hair, then stopped short, letting his hand fall to his side.

'What?' Storm almost smiled. 'Forget I had it cut?'

Blaze shook his head. 'No, forgot you've become a young man who probably doesn't appreciate it.'

Storm gave his best glare. 'I've never appreciated it. But don't waste your time. Go see if you can sort out some leave.'

He didn't miss Bonnie and Blaze's grins as they met each

other's gaze and turned. 'Love you, Storm.'

Love. He grunted again. Soppy, annoying people. Soppy, annoying, loveable people.

***

Prince couldn't believe what he was hearing. He stood in Deborah and Parker's office, his mouth hanging open. He managed to pull himself together.

'You think I should leave my *wife?* That's why you called me in?'

Deborah nodded. 'She's a hindrance to you, Prince. She is holding you back. Her rebellion toward God is clear.'

He couldn't speak. Something hurt somewhere deep down inside. Rachel had been right about them all along. He had come here to let them know he didn't think it would work to use an actor instead of Rachel and that he was standing by his decision to resign.

'You're not right for each other, Prince.' Parker had come to his side and put a hand on his shoulder. It was intended to be comforting but it burned through his shirt.

Maybe Parker was right. Maybe they weren't right for each other. But it wasn't because Rachel wasn't good enough for him. It was because he wasn't good enough for her. She hadn't been fooled the way he had.

Parker placed some papers in front of him. 'If you sign here, we can help you gain custody of your children. And I think you'll have to agree that Rebecca will match our image better.'

Prince felt like his heart was going to pound right out of his chest. 'You want me to marry Rebecca? Because you don't think Rachel's pretty enough?'

Deborah smiled. 'We want you to marry Rebecca because Rachel clearly isn't saved and God doesn't want his children to be unequally yoked.' Her lips tilted into a smug smile. 'Rebecca's very amenable to the idea, Prince. And she's always wanted twins.'

Prince felt sick. Anger filled him. Did they think they could buy him?

Deborah pushed on. 'It wasn't the right time to tell you, but in my vision of you walking away from your wife that day I met you in the hospital, you were walking toward Rebecca. It's always been God's plan.'

Prince couldn't speak. He looked at the papers drawn up in front of him. He looked again at the figure written down for his wages. It meant nothing to him without Rachel. Stepping forward, he picked up the papers, glared a direct challenge into Deborah and Parker's eyes and began to tear them up. One by one he let the pieces drop to the floor. His voice shook with rage and disgust.

'I'm sorry, I don't know what sort of man you think I am, but I have just realised we don't serve the same God. You are not welcome in my home. I'm going home to my *wife*, the wife God gave me, whom I love and happen to think is beautiful in every way possible.'

With that, he took a deep breath and left the building without looking back.

***

Rachel spent the afternoon trying to sort through her fears and emotions. Prince had been distant and she knew she had hurt him. It wasn't Prince she didn't trust, it was Rebecca. He deserved an apology and she needed to fight for him. God had given her a precious gift in her husband and she wasn't about to let misunderstanding get in the way of accepting that gift.

She had to explain why she thought the church was a cult. The more she thought about it, the more obvious it was. Deborah and Parker were controlling and their focus was on money, not God. It did seem they had God-given supernatural gifts, but they could be faked.

She heard a car come in the drive. Prince was home early. It was time she went to greet him the way she used to. Those first few months of marriage she had run to meet him every time he arrived home. These days she didn't even acknowledge him if she was busy with the twins.

She headed toward the door. It opened, and there he stood. He looked pale and shaken.

She reached out to put her arms around his neck and kiss him, but he pulled her to himself and clung to her.

'Prince? What's happened?'

She pulled back and looked up into his troubled eyes. He seemed unable to speak.

'Prince, I'm sorry.' She said the words quietly, afraid of the response, or maybe more afraid of no response. Had she created a rift between them could never be healed?

He shook his head and made his way to the lounge room on unsteady legs, lowering himself down onto the couch.

He couldn't even look at her. She drew a deep breath, her eyes welling with tears. 'I'm sorry for … well, for whatever is wrong with me.'

A strange expression passed over his face. 'You think there's something wrong with you?'

Her eyes dropped to the floor. '*You* think there's something wrong with me. Your church doesn't even think I know God, my closest friend.' Tears welled in her eyes as she spoke. When they cleared enough for her to see Prince's expression she stepped back. His mouth was set in a tight line.

Lord, we need your help. Please. I need to explain to him about the church.

But his eyes slid closed as though shutting her out. She turned to leave.

'Rachel. Wait.'

She turned back. 'Rach, you have to forgive me.' He reached out a hand and she moved toward him her heart pounding in her chest. Something was terribly wrong.

The moment she placed her hand in his, he pulled her down into his lap then gently turned her head to face him.

'I love you, Rachel.' His dark eyes begged her to believe him. 'I want you—not anyone else. Just you.'

Her eyes slid shut before the tears she had been holding back betrayed her and trailed in a river down her cheeks. He leaned his forehead against hers and just stayed there for a time. Then she felt his lips brush against hers.

'I've missed this. I've missed you,' she whispered. She forced herself to move closer, part of her wanting to and another part afraid. She still had to tell him she thought the church was a cult. Even if she told him, would he leave again as soon as his phone rang? Her eyes sprang open.

He was so close, looking at her so tenderly. 'It's just about driven me crazy, the distance between us,' he admitted, seeming to read her thoughts. 'Here is my wife right by my side and I don't even feel like I'm married anymore.'

Rachel put her arms around his waist, burying her head in his chest and feeling safe in his embrace. His hand came up to stroke her hair.

'Rach?' his voice was soft and deep.

'Yeah?'

'If we went back to our old church would you come?'

Her head came up. 'The uni church?'

'Yes.'

Could he mean it? Hope filled her like water filling an empty creek. She had missed the uni church when they moved to this new house. They had been married there—Prince had become a Christian there.

'Didn't we decide it's too far away from here?' she asked tentatively.

He nodded. 'We did, but it's only an hour. We could manage if you let me help you get the twins ready.'

She said nothing for a moment, mind and heart racing. Had God already shown Prince the Happy Kingdom Church was a cult? What had happened? She was afraid to ask.

'It's a long way to go. Could we try another church around here?'

He nodded. 'Good idea. But will you let me help with the twins?'

'You really want to?'

He looked sad. 'They're mine too. I want you to trust me with them.'

Her eyes widened. 'You think I don't trust you?'

'You won't let me help. I feel like you've been shutting me out.'

Rachel drew in a deep, shuddering breath. 'I thought you wouldn't want to help. You brought Kylie here. And Storm. And Parker and Deborah kept you so busy. I wanted you to feel free to work to provide for us.'

'Oh Rach, there's been so many misunderstandings. We need to be in this together.'

Suddenly her arms tightened around him. 'What about your job, Prince? It's your dream.'

He cut her off. 'No, you are my dream. To live for God and love my wife and children is my dream.'

The phone rang, startling both of them. She waited for him to jump up, but he didn't move. The answering machine kicked in.

'Prince? It's Parker. You need to face the truth. We prayed in faith, believing for healing, but your marriage is in deep trouble. You know that. We all know that. Call me.'

Rachel gasped, but Prince looked serene as he smiled into her eyes. 'I've faced the truth, Rach, and the truth is, I can't heal our marriage. I can't even force God to heal our marriage. There's not some formula of faith that makes God do what we want him to. God is God. It wasn't Deborah's prayers that healed you and our twins. It was God.'

'But Deborah says we're struggling because I lack faith.

Didn't she say I'm the reason our marriage is in trouble?'

Prince shook his head. 'Probably Deborah said that. But she's wrong. We're both struggling, Rach. But not because you lack faith. It's because I forgot what life is really all about. It's not about being blessed financially or having supernatural gifts or power or respect. It's about knowing Jesus and loving him and his people. Especially the family he's given me.'

Rachel broke down and Prince took her face in his hands. 'Rach, let's begin again. Let's go back to basics. We'll be poor and happy again. I'll go back to wearing jeans and holey old shirts and feel comfortable for the first time in weeks.'

Rachel nodded into his shirt, feeling hope flow within her veins. She wasn't alone anymore. They were together in their faith. When he lifted her chin and began to kiss her, she was no longer afraid. She felt such love for this man it overwhelmed her.

'Thank you, God,' she heard Prince whisper between kisses and she felt warm and safe. Everything was going to be okay.

<h1 style="text-align:center">Chapter Twelve</h1>

'Excuse me,' Tori tapped a lady on the arm. She turned, then stepped back, giving her a wary look. That's right, she was a ruffian now—a circus employee. Obviously, she had done a good job and looked the part with her wild mop of curls, ragged clothes and tanned skin. 'I'm looking for a circus.'

The lady frowned. 'Sorry, I can't help you.' She deliberately turned her back and Tori knew she needed to find another way. Centrelink. They often had a job search computer. Her mother had made her search them for modelling jobs.

'I'm looking for Centrelink,' she said to a passing man. He glanced at her, pointed down the street and kept walking. A few teens stood outside the front of a building ahead, some smoking, wearing beanies and looking much like the homeless she'd lived with a few weeks ago. It must be Centrelink. She walked in, feeling like she belonged. There were a few other people there, looking just like she did.

Her eyes scanned the room as she pulled Storm's resume from her small bag. She moved to the nearest free terminal and began typing in his details. He was a few years older than she was. That was a surprise. His photo made him look a lot younger. But then, maybe it was an old photo. She shook her head. As long as she didn't run into anyone who knew Storm she'd be fine.

He had worked in Marcos' circus so she needed to find a different one. Were there two in Australia? Or more? She wasn't sure.

It was clear circus performers were not the norm. None of the boxes the computer required her to tick really fit. Storm's job was clearly not clerical or medical, nor was it agricultural. Maybe animal care? That was about the closest it came.

To her disappointment, no circus jobs came up. Now she was at a loss. She couldn't help the cry of exasperation that escaped her lips.

'Are you right there?'

Tori almost jumped at the sound of the voice at her side. A lady from the Centrelink office was looking over her shoulder.

'I'm not, actually. I need to find a circus to get a job.'

The woman leaned over her shoulder and pointed to all the other suggestions and vacancies that had come up on the screen.

'What about these?'

Tori turned to face her, shaking her head. 'I need the circus. I've grown up in one and it's the only culture I can live in. I couldn't work inside, cleaning cages in a vet surgery. I would feel claustrophobic. And I'm not from this town, anyway.'

Lies and stories came more easily every time she told one. She'd watched her mother tell them expertly for years. Acting had always been one of Tori's strong points. Modelling required it.

The Centrelink officer studied Tori's troubled eyes and a look of sympathy came over her face. 'Give me a moment.' She went back to her desk and picked up her phone. When she returned she held out a piece of paper with a phone number and address on it.

'There's a circus at Segaldon at the moment. It's the only one I could track down. It's called "Brindley's".'

Tori could have hugged the woman. Things seemed to be working out for her even when it felt like there was no hope. First she had found the caravan, and now this woman had found a circus for her.

It was a five hour trip to Segaldon by car, but Tori believed she could catch a train as close as it went, and then hitchhike the last half hour or walk if necessary. If only she could get this job and settle into the circus life with food and shelter, she knew she would be okay. There was no room for dreams, hopes or plans.

She was now good at avoiding ticket collectors, so the train trip was uneventful. The final walk to the small town of Segaldon was the worst part. She put her thumb out to request a lift but no one stopped.

By the time she trudged up the second hill, she wished she had stolen some money from somewhere and caught a taxi. She was passing a gate with a deserted-looking mail box when a car drove from along the dirt road leading to it and stopped not far from her. A woman collected some mail, giving Tori a quick wave. Then she looked harder. 'You okay?'

Tori nodded, then changed her mind. 'Actually, no. I was riding to Segaldon, but my bike broke.'

'Broke?'

Tori searched her mind, quickly. 'Yeah, the chain snapped. Do you know of any way I can get into town? I'm with the circus, but I don't have my mobile phone with me.'

The woman smiled. 'I can drop you in,' she said in a friendly tone. 'That's if you don't mind catching a lift with a stranger. I need to go in and get a few groceries anyway.'

Relief filled her tired body in a wave. 'That would be great!' How was it that things were falling into place? It couldn't last long, surely. When would things start to fall apart again as they always did?

'I'm Cheryl,' said the woman as she started up the car and headed into town.

'Storm,' Tori said.

Cheryl glanced at her, then back to the road. 'Unusual name, but I like it.'

Tori didn't answer, but had to admit she liked it too.

'What do you do in the circus?'

'Not much. Just help out. My dad's into horses, that's why he named me after one.'

Tori found herself swallowing hard with each lie, her mind straining to keep up with them. She was tired and hungry and making up life stories was hard work.

'Your dad rides horses in the circus or cares for them?'

Tori knew nothing about riding and so thought the other option was safer. 'Cares for them.'

Cheryl smiled. 'A man after my own heart.'

Tori grew wary.

'What kind of horses do they use for the ring?'

Tori shrugged. 'It depends on what the rider works with best.'

The woman was insistent. 'Are thoroughbreds better for training? I always find them a bit more temperamental.' She grinned. 'I breed horses.'

Tori had feared as much. 'I'm not sure what kinds they use …' She wished she knew how to change the subject.

Cheryl fell quiet and the silence that followed was awkward. It was a few minutes before she spoke again.

'Look Storm, if that's your name, you have secrets you don't want to share with me and that's okay, but you don't have to try to make up stories for me.'

Tori's head jarred as she looked at her, then down again quickly.

Cheryl's eyes were focused on the road. 'I just want you to know that whatever you have done in your life, there is a way out.'

Tori couldn't help herself; she had to know. 'What do you mean?'

The woman looked at her, then pulled over. Tori saw that they had come to the circus.

'I mean God accepts you and will forgive, no matter what, if you ask him to. Never think you are alone, Storm. He's always there, just waiting to hear from you.'

Tori stared at her. She didn't understand why the eyes before her misted with tears. 'Storm, I see in your face that you are troubled. Lost. I admit I don't even know if you're a boy or a girl. You look like you need a good feed and somewhere safe. If this circus doesn't turn out to be the safe place you're running to, come back and talk to me. You saw where I live. My door is always open. And I am always ready to share the love of Jesus.'

Tori looked into the warm kindness of her eyes. 'The Jesus of the Bible?'

She nodded. 'Jesus, who is alive today, who loves you.'

Loved her? Nobody had ever loved her. Except maybe Sarah but Sarah was gone. She forced down the lump in her throat. She couldn't afford to think about Sarah. Even her own mother couldn't love and accept her. She knew enough about Jesus from what she'd learned in school Scripture to know he was supposedly God. How could he love her? It didn't make sense. But she had to find a job.

Cheryl was still looking at her with that tender, concerned look.

'Thank you,' Tori whispered, not knowing what else to say. Then she gave a quick wave and walked toward the circus tent. Here her new life would begin, if only no one realised she wasn't Storm.

Chapter Thirteen

Prince stood tall and reached out his hand for Rachel's. She'd picked this church as the first local one to try. She glanced at him, back to the church building, then wrapped her fingers around his.

'Back to the Gospel,' she whispered.

He drew in a deep breath. Yes, the Gospel. The belief her parents had died for. The friendship with God that was all about love, not demands and obligations.

She gave him a troubled look. 'It feels wrong without the twins.'

'I know. But they're safe with Kylie.' He squeezed her hand, then pulled her closer. 'Let's do this together.'

She nodded and fell into step beside him.

The man at the door smiled and welcomed them, looking genuinely delighted to see them.

No mints were given out, and there was no glossy church newsletter for the week. Only the gentle sound of organ music and the calm chatter of the congregation could be heard wafting from inside. They headed in.

An elderly couple nodded and smiled at them as they slid into pews. Then the couple in front of them turned around. The woman smiled. 'Welcome. I'm Carol and this is my husband, Tom.'

'I'm Prince and this is my wife, Rachel.'

The woman looked so different to Deborah. There was nothing exceptional about her features and she wore plain clothes, but there was something beautiful about her. He realised what it was. She had an open, caring expression and a joy that shone through her eyes. She reached out and touched Rachel's arm. 'I believe you are the couple we've been praying for.'

Rachel's eyes widened and Prince felt his heart sink. Here, too? Were this couple going to try to manipulate them into their church?

Tom was nodding. 'Carol came to me and said she had a dream. In it, she saw a couple here at church; a couple God is going to use in mighty ways. They welcomed a girl into their home who was alone in the world and needed to hear the Gospel.'

Prince frowned. 'I'm not sure you've got the right people. We're busy caring for our own twin babies right now.'

Carol smiled, undeterred, and her eyes shone. 'Look to Jesus. He is the one who has your best interests at heart. And when you do, you will reach many with Jesus' love. Your home will be filled with the broken and hurting, but there they will find Jesus and be restored.'

Prince glanced at Rachel. He couldn't tell what she thought, but she seemed comfortable and happy. She began chatting with Carol, telling her about the twins.

He glanced around the room, not knowing what to think. It was so different from the modern church building of the Happy Kingdom Church. There were no luxurious chairs to relax in here; not that much time had been spent in the chairs.

He remembered Deborah the first day he'd stepped into the Happy Kingdom Church. She had raced to him, speaking a word of knowledge over him and announcing in a loud voice that this man needed prayer, as he was overwhelmed with trouble. Prince had had a mint thrust into his hand and had soon felt strangely uninhibited. He had opened up to them about Rachel. The whole church had gathered around him in the doorway and prayed. The prayer support was exactly what he'd been longing for. He'd been overwhelmed by the intensity of the people and had appreciated it at the time. Now he knew they had used his need and manipulated him.

But in this place, there was no intensity, no overwhelming emotion, no immediate meeting of a need … but time to think.

The congregation began by singing 'Be still and know that I am God'. Prince smiled at the thought of the Happy Kingdom Church ever singing this way. The song seemed to drag but if Rachel was happy here he could cope.

A lady came to the front for a Bible reading. Prince closed his eyes and listened. She was reading from Psalm 42, that same verse from the Bible and he found himself soaking it up. *Be still and know that I am God.* Amidst all the noise of life, the effort of trying to be who God wanted him to be, the crying babies, he'd forgotten his relationship with God.

He glanced at Rachel. Her eyes were misty. She caught his gaze, then leaned over and whispered in his ear. 'Dad loved that verse. And we sang that song in church.'

The full impact of her words sunk in. She was being reminded of her childhood and the love and faith of her parents who gave their lives on the mission field. He knew Rachel had once loved the times spent alone with God when she would write songs and poems for him and spend hours just talking with God, enjoying his presence.

A man came to the front and opened his Bible, ready to give the sermon. Prince leaned forward, listening intently, longing to hear the Gospel, to know it and understand once again.

But he was disappointed. The sermon was a challenge to reach out to others with the Gospel, but there was no mention of what it was. And as people introduced themselves and said hello afterwards, he didn't have the courage to ask. He appreciated their love, but even this church didn't offer what he was looking for. Whatever that was.

*****

Tori hadn't thought it would be so hard to get a job.

'I can't take you on as my employee, Storm!' Her potential boss paced his van, looking perplexed. 'Everybody who knows anybody in a circus has heard of you.' He pointed to Storm's resume. 'And your old boss already hates me. In fact, if Marcos wasn't in jail I wouldn't be game to even talk to you. Can you imagine if I took his best ring performer and made even more competition for him?'

Immediately Tori relaxed. 'Oh, I don't want to ride! I just miss the circus life and don't want to go back with Marcos. Give me a job cleaning cages. That will be enough.'

Max Brindley looked at her as if he didn't believe what he just heard. 'Cage cleaning? You can't be serious! What a waste, boy! You're too talented for that.'

'Please.' Tori begged and Max looked at her suspiciously.

'What do you really want from me?'

'Just a job in the environment I love.'

Max scrutinised her from under bushy eyebrows then finally shrugged. 'Okay. But if you get me into trouble ...'

'I won't, I promise. I'll just clean those cages and mind my own business. Nobody will even see me.'

Max still didn't look convinced. 'I suppose you have your own accommodation.'

She hadn't thought of that. Of course Storm would have taken his caravan wherever he went. 'No.' She tried to think of a suitable reason. 'I, um, I loaned it to a friend and they trashed it.'

Max frowned. 'You really are in a bad spot, aren't you? Well, you can use one of our spares. It's nothing fancy but it'll keep you dry. Hang on, I'll get you a key.' He went to a filing cabinet and scrabbled around until he came back with one. He held it out to Tori. 'You know, I guess it wouldn't hurt for you to work with some of my horses, train them for me.'

'I can't do that.' Tori cut him off with forced cheerfulness. 'Marcos would hate both of us then. Not worth the risk.'

Max grinned. 'Good point.' Then he frowned. 'If you're spying on me or something ...'

'I'm not!' Tori looked directly into his eyes. 'I told you, I haven't even seen Marcos for years.' At least that much was true.

Max nodded. 'I know. I heard all about the fight between you Clements kids and Marcos on the news. Okay, you have a job, but just to put it out there, I know you're not giving me the full story. But if you're not running from the law or causing me trouble, I'll let you have your secrets.'

Relief filled Tori, and even when she was led to a dirty old caravan she wasn't bothered. At least she had space to herself and a roof over her head. Her first pay-day would be in a week and she would have food to eat. That was all she asked.

***

The doorbell screamed and Prince sighed. Every time someone came to the door he dreaded it would be Deborah and Parker. They'd been phoning incessantly. Why couldn't they respect his decision? He was exhausted after a morning at church and really didn't want to deal with them right now.

He swung open the door and his face fell. There they stood, dressed in all their finery, their faces set.

'We need to see you and your wife.'

He toyed with closing the door in their faces. No, he needed to be mature. God loved them. He would love them too, but he would be cautious. 'Parker. Deborah. How are you?'

Deborah looked him up and down. 'Your clothes?'

He glanced down at his casual tee-shirt and jeans and smiled. 'I haven't found more work yet. No need for dressing up.'

Parker frowned. 'While you were under the banner of God's church you had everything you needed. I don't understand …'

Prince shrugged. 'Rachel prefers me in these.'

Deborah stepped in front of her husband. 'We've been concerned that you have completely cut us off. You can't let your wife convince you to turn your back on God. He doesn't let backsliders go unpunished.' Her tone was blunt, demanding an explanation.

Prince frowned. 'I thought I made it clear. I don't believe as you do and I will never leave Rachel.

Parker rubbed the back of his neck. 'Yes, well, maybe we didn't explain ourselves properly.'

What could there be to explain? He looked at them steadily, waiting. A movement behind him caught his attention and he turned to see Rachel there looking awkward. He reached a hand to her, wishing he could take the uncertain look from her eyes. They were in this together. He needed her right now and she needed him. He grasped her hand as she reached his side. 'Rachel and I are doing well. You don't need to worry about us.'

'But you've rejected the church.'

He was relieved when Rachel spoke up. 'No, not the church as a whole. We just believe differently to your organisation.'

Prince nodded. 'For now we are seeking God and finding him in the quiet stillness of our home and hearts.'

Deborah and Parker looked as though he had slapped them in the face. It was Parker who regained his thoughts first. 'Prince, coming to church is essential. Without it, a believer dies. You need our support, you need to come into the presence of God and enter where his Spirit dwells.'

Rachel smiled at them. 'Prince isn't saying we won't be finding a church to be part of. We know it's important. But God's Spirit dwells within us, his people, not a church building.'

Prince nodded. 'We're looking for a church who share our faith and whose focus is love and what Jesus has done for us.'

Immediately Deborah began praying in tongues and Parker tried to lay his hands on Prince. He backed away. Rachel was right. He wasn't going to find God in their church. God dwelt within him. God was already here, just waiting for him to call on him.

'Prince, you must not be unequally yoked!' Parker said urgently, his wife still muttering in the background and a child beginning to cry from one of the bedrooms. 'Your wife is a snare to you. You must reject all that is unholy and all she stands for. Your mind is being corrupted by the spirit of contempt within her.'

Rachel's lip began to tremble and anger rose up within Prince at their disrespect for her. He raised his voice above their babble. 'I'd like you to leave now.'

They ignored him and he felt himself standing taller, his mouth forming a grim line. 'Leave my house!' He was all but shouting now. 'You have no right to come here and insult Rachel!'

The babbling stopped and Parker rubbed the back of his neck again, looking stressed. 'We are concerned for your soul, Prince.'

Prince's voice quietened. 'No, you are concerned about being right. You have shown no love to Rachel or anyone who doesn't believe what you do.'

With that, he shut the door. He sat down on the lounge, head in his hands. He felt empty, lost and desperate. 'Help me, God!'

A gentle hand touched his arm. 'He is, Prince. And thank you.'

He turned to look into her warm brown eyes. 'For what?'

'Standing up for me.'

He drew her head against his chest and stroked her hair. 'Oh Rach, what else would I do? I love you. You're my wife.'

She looked up into his eyes and smiled and it was then he knew. God had healed their marriage.

***

'Here, let me.' Prince took the clean nappy from Rachel's hands and moved to the change table where Seton lay. Compassion shone from his eyes. 'You're wrecked.'

She gave him a half-hearted smile. 'So are you.'

His arm came around her. 'It's just a season. We'll get through this.'

She nodded and watched as he began to change Seton and chatter to him. The little boy gave him a huge smile and it warmed her heart. He was a good father and he finally had time to be one.

The doorbell rang and both she and Prince jarred. Seton's face began to screw up, but Prince smiled at him and started talking again. Why couldn't people leave them alone? She was so tired of visitors. She should get the door, but Prince was ignoring it. She would take her cue from him. Kylie could get it if she wanted to. It was probably Parker and Deborah coming back, trying a new tack to get Prince to come back to their church. At what point could it be considered harassment?

Muffled voices came through the wall and Rachel saw the way Prince stood completely still, straining to hear. Then he began to smile. Grabbing Seton up from the change table, he raced out of the room. Rachel stared after him. Clearly he recognised the voices and clearly it wasn't Deborah and Parker now in their lounge room talking to Kylie.

Picking up Blythe from where she lay contentedly in her cot, she followed him out the door.

Kylie stood in the lounge room and by her side, was Prince's brother Blaze, and his wife, Bonnie.

'Blaze!' Prince passed the baby to Kylie and moved straight past her to reach his brother.

He banged Blaze enthusiastically on the back while Blaze threw Rachel a tentative look. 'Had to come and visit. I know you said not to yet, but ...' He shrugged.

Prince grinned. 'We don't mind visitors like this, do we Rach?'

She smiled. 'No.' Anyone who brought Prince such joy was welcome any time. He looked alive again as he took Blythe from her arms and shoved her into Blaze's. 'Meet your niece.'

Blaze looked taken aback, but pulled himself together when Bonnie came to his side and began talking to the baby in his arms. Blythe gurgled and smiled, putting on a perfect performance.

*****

Prince watched his brother and sister-in-law as they gushed over the twins and he smiled. Storm could learn from them. But then, Storm didn't have the open, compassionate heart Blaze and Bonnie did. Storm didn't know God the way Blaze and Bonnie did.

Blaze and Bonnie were like Rachel. As far as he knew they didn't speak in tongues or have the gift of healing or prophecy or any obvious supernatural gift that they made a big show of. Love was what was so supernatural about them.

They were the type of Christians he wanted to be. He had felt confused by Deborah and Parker and he still had so many questions. Clearly, that was why God had brought them.

Rachel was playing the perfect hostess. 'Have a seat. Can I get you a tea or coffee?'

He didn't wait for them to answer. He looked directly across at them as they settled into the chair. 'I know why you're here.'

His cryptic comment didn't seem to surprise either of them. Blaze just looked steadily back at him. 'Why are we here?'

Prince lowered himself into the spare armchair. 'God brought you because I need to hear the Gospel again. You've studied it, Blaze. You know it inside out. I need to hear it. Not all the side issues. Just the basics.'

Blaze's eyes widened slightly before understanding seemed to fill his eyes. He leaned forward in his chair. 'All you have to do is believe, Prince.'

Prince frowned. Surely he wasn't going to leave it at that? Rachel moved to sit on the arm of his chair and gave him an understanding look. He appreciated her support.

'Believe in what, Blaze? In tongues as a sign of salvation? In Baptism? In healing? Gifts? Blessings as a sign of God's favour?'

He wasn't aware of the way he waved his arms about, until she saw Bonnie's look of surprise. Everyone was looking at him, probably wondering why he hadn't asked his own wife. After all, she was the daughter of a minister, grounded in her faith, dependable and all-together. The truth was, he hadn't wanted to disappoint her; to admit he was confused. But now his need was stronger than his pride.

'It's simple,' Blaze said quietly. 'Those things you've just mentioned can make it all so complicated.'

'Then what is it?' Prince asked, grasping Rachel's hand as he leaned forward. 'Spell it out for me!'

Blaze met Prince's eyes before looking directly at Rachel. 'It's just as your father taught, Rachel. That God loved the world so much he sent his only son to die so that if you believe in him you will live forever. John 3:16.'

Prince frowned. 'Okay, we believe in him, so we can live forever after we die, but what about now? How do we live for him now? How do we know we are truly his?'

But Rachel cut him off, her eyes filled with excitement. 'That's just it, Prince! We don't have to do anything. We don't even have to understand all those things like supernatural gifts. We just need to believe in Jesus and know and love him.'

'But is that all? Is that enough?'

'That's the Gospel!' Rachel laughed, jumping up from the chair and releasing his hand. He missed its warmth but her face was shining. 'Not that we're worthy or can live in a way that makes ourselves worthy. That's the whole point, remember? That's why I wore white at our wedding even though we'd messed up so bad. We're not good enough and can't be, so Jesus Christ took our place and made us perfect in his sight.'

It was true, Prince knew that. But it still didn't answer his questions about the gifts and the outward signs of salvation.

Blaze was watching him closely, his expression gentle. 'Prince, Paul in the Bible had the gift of tongues, but he also said they have their place. Do you know the verse in 1 Corinthians

13? Hang on …' He pulled his phone from his pocket and began scrolling through.

'Here it is. Paul says, *If I speak with the tongues of men and of angels, but do not have love, I have become a noisy gong or a clanging cymbal. If I have the gift of prophecy, and know all mysteries and all knowledge; and if I have all faith, so as to remove mountains, but do not have love, I am nothing. And if I give all my possessions to feed the poor, and if I surrender my body to be burned, but do not have love, it profits me nothing...*'

Prince nodded slowly. 'So all those things are good, but if we do them without love and for the wrong reason, then they are not from God.'

'Yes. They are God-given gifts to encourage Christians. We use them to worship and glorify God, to build each other up—'

They all started as the phone rang. Prince glanced at the caller ID and let out a laugh. 'Deborah. There is our clanging gong right there. That's what's missing with them, Rach. Love.'

Bonnie shifted Blythe to her shoulder and leaned forward. 'In John 13:35 Jesus said that we'll know who his children are by the love we have for one another. And we can only show that love if we truly belong to God.'

***

Kylie sat in the next room, listening to the conversation. It made so much sense. How could Prince not get it?

She shook her head in exasperation. How much simpler did Blaze need to make it? Frustration rose within her and she wished she could yell at Prince; to make him see.

Just believe in Jesus, Prince! Like Rachel does. Trust him with your life!

Something shifted in her heart. For years she'd watched her cousin live for Christ and seem mature way beyond her years.

111

She'd watched her live a 'good' life and care for people naturally. She'd felt frustration when Rachel refused to go to discos or parties with her, when she had worn less than fashionable clothing, when her reserved nature had made her the centre of class jokes. Now it suddenly became clear. All those things weren't 'being a Christian'. Believing in Jesus was being a Christian.

It wasn't beyond Kylie Sandom after all. Even Kylie could believe! And so silently, without any witnesses apart from God himself, Kylie asked for forgiveness and believed.

'I will live for you, now, God,' she prayed. 'I'm tired of living for myself anyway.'

There would be no more travelling the world in search of purpose and identity. There would be no more restlessness or helplessness. Kylie Sandom had found her place in the world, or rather, in God's loving arms.

She watched through the door as Prince took one of the twins in his arms and smiled, completely at peace. Everything was okay now. It was time for her to go.

CHAPTER FOURTEEN

Rachel stood beside Prince, looking out their window, enjoying the morning sunrise after the rain. It was a day of new beginnings for them and they'd begun it in prayer. God loved them. He'd never disowned them, despite their disillusionment, their mistakes and failures.

'Rachel, even when I was so lost and confused, God never let me go,' Prince said in wonder. He drew her into his arms. 'I forgot him and Satan nearly had me, but God didn't forget me and he held on to me.'

Rachel smiled up at him. 'It's like when Noah was in the ark and the Bible says "God remembered Noah". Noah must have started to wonder. The rain went on for so long.'

Prince nodded. 'And then there was the rainbow. A sign of God's promise to Noah.' He pulled Rachel closer. 'Rach, from now on I'm going to remember it's not about us clinging to the cross, but about Christ holding onto us.'

Rachel smiled. 'Let's cling to that promise!'

As they gazed out the window, Prince pointed up into the sky. 'Look.'

And she smiled in delight, for there was a magnificent rainbow on the horizon.

'God's promises are rainbows in the storms of life,' she said quietly, then pulled out of Prince's arms and rushed to her bedside. She pulled out a pen and piece of paper.

'What are you doing?' Prince asked in amusement.

'A poem just came to me. I have to write it down.'

His eyes twinkled at her. 'The Rachel I know and love is back!'

***

Storm Clements left his caravan on the roads, seething with anger. Someone had cleaned out all the food while he was away. Then to top it off, he had been fired! He couldn't believe the attitude of his boss. True, he had returned a day late, but it was a family emergency. But his arrogant, heartless employer refused to listen. He'd cut him off with a mocking laugh as though the thought of Storm Clements caring about his family was a joke. Storm kicked at a rock. Did he really come across as so uncaring?

His phone buzzed in his pocket and he pulled it out. Prince. He wasn't surprised. He had known Prince would eventually call to apologise.

'You're forgiven.' He knew he snapped the words, but he wanted to get the formalities and all the emotional stuff over with.

A deep, throaty chuckle came back at him. 'Thank you. So are you.'

Storm frowned. 'What for? For stopping myself knocking some sense into you?'

'No. For sending visitors our way even though Rachel said she didn't want them.'

So Blaze and Bonnie had visited. 'Did they help?' He couldn't stop the hopeful tone in his voice.

'Yes. Rachel and I have discovered you just have to wait for the rain to stop. And while the storm is raging you have to cling to the promise of the rainbow.'

'Don't go all poetic on me. You know I don't have time for it.'

'It's not a poem. Although Rachel has made it into one now.'

He grunted. 'No doubt she'll turn it into a song next.'

'No doubt.'

'She must be happy again, then.'

'Yes. I've left the Happy Kingdom Church. Best thing I ever did, apart from marrying Rachel. And giving my life to God, of course.'

Storm was surprised at the intensity of relief that washed over him. But Prince's next words threw him.

'So we're happy now. Are you?'

Happy? Happiness wasn't something he expected to find for himself, though he realised he wanted Prince and Rachel to have it. 'I've lost my job.'

'Oh? What will you do? You can stay here for a while. I don't know what you'd do with Dusty Lane and your caravan, though. We don't really have room for a horse and van here.'

'Nah. Thanks for the offer, but I think I'll go back to the circus.' Even as he spoke the words they filled him with hope. He realised then that his heart had never really left the circus. He loved performing. He loved the expressions he saw in the faces of those watching him; the wide-eyed wonder and admiration.

'But Storm, as if they'd take you back after everything that's happened. Marcos isn't happy with us.'

'Marcos is in jail.'

'Yes, but our sister put him there. And his son is probably in charge now.'

'Probably, but Chase isn't stupid. Everyone has heard of us, Prince. All he'd have to do is advertise that one of the Clements family is back in the ring and he'd have a full house.'

There was silence for a moment before Prince's voice quietly acknowledged the truth of his words. Then he said, 'I hope you find the fulfilment you're searching for.'

'Thank you, dear brother.' Storm's words were laced with sarcasm as he finished the call, but he appreciated Prince's words just the same. He was tired of the restlessness that had led him from one venture to another all his life.

***

It wasn't Marcos' son Chase, but his younger son, Clay who came out to meet Storm as he arrived on Dusty Lane. Clay looked years older and had a confidence in his stance he had never had as a child. Storm dismounted. 'I'm here to see Chase.'

'Chase left years ago. Became a policeman.'

Storm narrowed his eyes. That was unlikely. 'Who's in charge then?'

'Me. What can I do for you?'

Storm was taken aback. It would have been easier to deal with Chase than Clay. Clay had good reason to dislike him. Oh well, it was worth a try.

'I want to work here again. I want you to take me back.'

Clay seemed lost for words. He opened his mouth, shut it again then sputtered. 'Take you back?' Red crept up his neck and into his face until he looked like he might explode. 'What, cage cleaning didn't suit you?'

Storm frowned. What was he talking about? 'Cage cleaning?'

Clay shook his head. 'You Clements kids always were too high and mighty for your own good. Well, all I can say is it serves you right. Go back to Brindley and smear your face in his animal dung again. I don't want you here!'

Storm grabbed Clay by the arm and he saw a brief moment of fear in the man's eyes. Quickly he let him go, remembering he was no longer the small boy who had once worked for this man's father. He didn't want to threaten him, just get answers. 'What are you talking about?'

Clay laughed a sneering laugh. 'First you put my Dad in jail—'

'That wasn't me. It was my sister.'

'Didn't see you try to stop it. Don't know what Dad saw in you. You always were his favourite.'

Storm was stunned into silence. Memories flashed through

116

his mind. Young Clay on the ground, knees scraped, crying. Marcos shoving him, knocking him off balance and telling him to get up and stop being such a girl.

'Look at Storm,' Marcos had said, his face showing his disgust at his son. 'Do you see him crying? He hurt himself way worse than you did when he fell off his horse. I've got no time for you and your drama.'

Storm remembered the way Marcos had called him to follow, told him how tough he was, how much better than his brothers and sisters he was. For a small boy lost in the midst of twins and triplets who were admired by anyone who set eyes on them, Storm had soaked up Marcos' words. Now he loathed them.

He tried to focus on Clay. 'What were you saying about Brindley?'

'You're not Dad's favourite anymore. He went ballistic when he heard you went to Brindley and asked for a job cleaning cages.'

'What?' Storm could hardly breathe.

'I know.' Clay chuckled. 'How could the famous Storm Clements sink so low?' He frowned. 'I have to admit I just don't get it. I know I was jealous of you as a kid, but we're adults now.' He took a deep breath. 'You have all the qualities and talents of a real performer. And you look even more impressive now than when we were kids!'

Storm laughed gruffly. 'What are you talking about? It's been years since I rode in a ring.'

'Maybe, but performing is something you never forget how to do, especially when it's in your blood. But I'm talking about your appearance. You were made to be admired. You're not a skinny little kid anymore. I'm surprised Brindley didn't put you in the ring.'

Storm ran a hand through his dark hair and shook his head. 'I'll have you know, Clay, that I would never lower myself to being a cleaner and I have no idea why Brindley is making up those stories for you. I've never met the man.' He stood straighter. 'But I'm going to meet him now!'

Clay stepped forward, his eyes softening. 'One more thing, Storm.'

He stopped, waiting.

'All the things Dad used to say, they're not necessarily true.'

Storm's brows shot up. What things? Marcos said so many things he couldn't possibly imagine what Clay was talking about.

'Your sister. Misty. I know he told you that you caused that scar on her face.'

Storm nodded. 'I got angry and pushed her off the railing, then laughed about it. I'm sick of hearing it.'

Clay's eyes dropped and he looked sad, almost sympathetic. Storm hated the feeling beginning somewhere down in his stomach.

Then his eyes looked directly into Storm's. 'Do you remember it?'

'Remember it actually happening? Of course not. I was only two.'

'She fell. All by herself. She fell asleep.'

He stared. He didn't want to believe it, but something in Clay's eyes told him he wasn't making it up. 'What about Dad? Did I —'

Clay shook his head. 'You didn't kick him in the face.'

'So why did Marcos say I did?'

'Dad always wanted a son just like him. I failed him. Chase failed him too – had too strong a sense of justice. Police work suits him perfectly. Anyway, I guess Dad thought he'd try to make you just like him. If you didn't measure up, he'd make you *think* you were just like him. He's not a nice man, Storm.'

'Why are you telling me this?'

Clay shrugged. 'I don't need to fight for who I am these days. I own this circus and I love it. Dad's in jail. I should actually be thanking you for that. He can't control me anymore.'

Storm didn't know what to think. He had worked out his identity based on what Marcos had told him. The man had taught him to take pride in being tough. That meant being cold and heartless. Storm had found security in being that way. That's why he would never resort to something like cage cleaning in Brindley's circus.

He had no idea what was going on, but he was determined to find out. His pride was injured almost more than he could bear. A cage cleaner! He was born to be a star. He had always known that; Marcos had made sure he knew that. But now he found himself questioning anything Marcos ever said or did, not to mention his own identity.

But the thought of anyone believing he would be a cage cleaner both infuriated and repulsed him. For some reason, Brindley had decided to mock him this way. Although, Storm wouldn't put it past Marcos to make the whole thing up just to get back at him. Marcos had been furious when the Clements family left his circus, taking their horses with them. They were the best in the country and the controlling man didn't want to let them go. He had caused as much trouble for them as he could and ended up in jail for his attempts at stealing the horses.

Storm had thought it was all over once it had gone through the courts but now he wasn't so sure.

Chapter Fifteen

Brindley's circus was far smaller than the circus Storm had spent his childhood in. The moment he saw the small array of caravans and trailers and the tent half the size of the one in Marcos', he knew there was no real competition between the two. Marcos or Clay must have made the whole story up.

'Excuse me,' Storm approached one of the maintenance men working on the tent.

The man looked up and then immediately stood and straightened. Marcos had once told him people did that because he had such a strong presence about him it commanded respect. But Marcos also told him he had scarred his sister for life.

'I'm Storm Clements. I'm looking for—'

'Storm?' the man cut him off, looking confused. 'You're not Storm. That's Storm.'

He pointed toward the tiger cage where a boy in overalls leaned over a water bowl, scrubbing it out. Storm stared, feeling as though he were looking at a younger version of himself. The boy wore ragged, baggy clothes, but his hair was unruly and his method haphazard.

He turned and Storm saw the side of his face. Definitely not his own! He took a deep breath and headed toward the cage.

The boy started as he appeared at his side. His eyes looked haunted and troubled, and Storm hated the vulnerability he saw there. This boy was pretending to be him, but doing a poor job of it. There was a weakness in the boy's troubled look that he despised.

'The maintenance man said you're Storm,' he said, trying to keep his anger at bay.

The boy didn't even flinch. 'That's right. Storm Clements.'

His arrogance was infuriating. He glared angrily at him. 'You're lying.'

The boy stood taller, an impassive expression on his face, though his voice became challenging. 'How dare you? You don't know what you're talking about.'

Storm smiled a dry, hard smile. 'I know you can't be who you claim to be.'

'Why not?'

'Because *I'm* Storm Clements.'

The eyes before him widened in fear for a moment, then the boy dropped the water bowl he was cleaning, his muscles tensed and ready for flight. But with reflexes like lightning, Storm had him pinned against the wall of the cage with his hands behind his back.

He gave him a rough shake and spoke gruffly into his ear. 'Tell me what's going on or I'll break both your arms and you'll never clean out another cage again.'

***

Tori had played her game so well until now she had developed a false sense of security. The real Storm Clements was the last person she'd expected to see as she cleaned the tiger cage that afternoon. She was well practised at hiding her emotions, but Storm's appearance had shocked her.

He was a fine-looking young man, nothing like the reckless teenager with the messy hairstyle and feminine features she'd impersonated. He stood tall above her small frame. Now she was still and silent, shocked by how strong and fast he was. There was no escape when he held her like this.

'How dare you ruin my reputation like that?' His teeth were gritted and she could see he was seething with anger.

She began to struggle, wondering what put this sudden fight in her. In all her years of helplessness beneath her mother's abuse, never had she been foolish enough to struggle. But Storm had her firm in his steely grip.

'Who are you?' His deep voice was rough and he twisted her arm until she winced. She continued to struggle despite the pain, until Storm threw her hard onto the ground. She let out a gasp, realising she was no match for him, and yet, she would rather die than be discovered. He couldn't force her to say anything she didn't want to. She had a high tolerance for pain.

***

Storm stared hard at the boy on the ground before him. He reached down, grabbed the skinny hand and lifted him roughly to his feet, and dragged him toward the Big Top. He could fight as long and hard as this insolent boy could.

'You're going to confess to these people that you're not who you claim to be. You're going to clear my name.'

The boy shook his head stubbornly. 'You can hurt me, but you can never force words out of my mouth.'

'Can't I?' He studied the boy's face, seeing something that shook him. His face had become hard and closed, almost disconnected from what was happening. 'Well, I know someone who knows you are not who you claim to be. Let's go on a little trip to Marcos' circus, shall we? Though I'm sure you already know where it is. He put you up to this, didn't he?'

He gasped. 'You're kidnapping me?'

The gasp indicated fear but when Storm stopped and looked into the clear green eyes he saw a blankness that surprised him. He shook his head. 'No. I'm just taking you for a ride.'

Storm had left Dusty Lane with Clay and brought his car, but being back in the circus made him desperate to ride. Let this boy experience a horse ride with the real Storm Clements. He dragged him to where the horses stood grazing peacefully nearby and looked them over. It didn't take him long to work out which one would make the trip.

Holding the boy tightly, arms pinned behind his bony back, Storm pushed him up onto the horse then swung up behind him effortlessly. The horse moved off at a gallop. These animals always trusted him.

Storm heard the shouts of several circus men as he 'stole' one of their horses, but his anger defied his conscience. Let those people pay for believing this weed of a boy was the great Storm Clements!

Chapter Sixteen

Tori was terrified and Storm's grip on her arms hurt. She struggled to stay upright on the horse and almost lost her balance several times but he held her firm.

When the circus was no longer in sight, he slowed the horse to a canter. Tori felt his hesitation and wondered what was happening. Then he stopped and lifted her down, his movements no longer aggressive and rough. She wondered what he was doing, as those dark eyes studied her intently.

'You're not with Marcos, are you?'

She just stared.

'You can't even ride, can you?"

Still she didn't respond.

'Are you with the circus?'

Her silence infuriated him and she saw his fist fly toward her. In the second before it struck she allowed herself to fall to the ground. She curled up in a tight ball, hands over her head, shutting out the world and breathing hard.

Nothing happened for so long she finally looked up. To her surprise, Storm was no longer standing over her, but had lowered himself to the ground where he squatted, staring at her, his eyes awash with confusion.

'What's all this about?' His voice was deep and hushed. She gazed at him, wishing she could trust him, but knowing she was on her own. Nobody could be trusted, not even this circus boy who looked so capable and in control.

***

Storm studied the blank green eyes. He was sure a haunted, troubled look had passed through them just a moment ago. How could somebody have so little expression? Something was going on here that he couldn't understand.

This boy was so arrogant, and yet at the same time, terrified. It was almost as though he believed his name truly was Storm. He genuinely seemed confused by any mention of Marcos. And then there was his reaction to his attempt to strike him. Storm had incredibly fast reflexes, but this boy ducked as though he were ready to be attacked at any moment. He'd never seen someone retreat so fast, nor someone so skilled at avoiding a blow.

He realised this boy was used to violence. With that revelation, his own anger diffused as quickly as it had come.

He noticed for the first time the scar down the boy's arm. It was similar to the one he had received when he fell of his horse onto bitumen as a four year old; the incident Marcos so often used to taunt his son. Storm hadn't cried. Somehow, he suspected this boy hadn't cried either. However, his scar looked new; stitch lines still showed across its jagged edges.

'Tell me what's going on,' he said again, this time in a gentler voice. 'Who are you?'

The clear green eyes before him looked calculating. He noticed it a moment too late as the boy saw his opportunity and ran.

Storm chased him as fast as he dared through the streets. Cars slowed, allowing him past, but the skinny boy was fast. He watched as he ducked around a corner and disappeared.

With a shrug, Storm gave up the chase. He could have tried to follow but he didn't want to leave the magnificent circus horse in the middle of nowhere and get in trouble for theft. Besides,

125

he didn't know what he'd do if he caught the kid anyway. He couldn't force anyone to talk and abduction was illegal.

He was probably just seeking opportunities in life that he didn't think he could find on his own. He headed back to the circus, preparing to explain what was going on to Max Brindley.

Max had gathered all the circus people together to formulate a plan to get their horse and 'Storm' back. Police were the last option for any circus employee, so Storm was met not with police, but wide-eyed circus people who knew the moment they saw him he was a performer and a skilled one.

'Sorry to take your horse.' He rode into the middle of the group and circled the horse. 'I can assure you he's not harmed.'

Still no one spoke, and Storm couldn't help a boyish grin forming on his face. 'I should introduce myself. I am the real Storm Clements. I don't know who that boy was you had here, but he's no circus performer.'

Still the group appeared speechless and he couldn't help enjoying the respect and admiration he saw in their eyes as he stood on the horse's back. He'd always loved it as a child and it had never quite left him.

'I'd like to work for you as a performer once I find out what that kid was doing using my name.' He searched their faces to work out which one was Max Brindley.

Max stepped forward, looking up at Storm, high on the horse. 'You would work for me?' Hope and disbelief mixed in his expression.

He nodded, doing a double backflip from the horse's back and landing nimbly on his feet directly in front of Max. He shook the stunned man's hand. 'I'll even forgive you for mistaking me to me some ragged little kid.' He felt his mouth tilt at the corners but stopped short of a full smile.

Brindley nodded. 'I like you, Storm. And I don't care what Marcos thinks. I've seen you ride now and there's no way I'm going to pass up your offer.'

Storm went through the boy's caravan, searching his possessions for any indication of who he might be or where he came from. All he found was an old blanket bunched in the corner of the bed. Shaking it, he watched in surprise as papers fell out.

'That's his resume. I mean, yours.' Brindley spoke from behind him. 'That's what he showed me. I didn't know any better.'

He studied the resume, then looked down at something on the bed. It was a small photo of him. He picked it up. 'That's an old one.'

Brindley came closer and took a look. He grinned sheepishly at Storm. 'Well, the kid didn't do too bad a job at impersonating you in the looks department.'

Storm grunted. 'I was never that skinny.' He picked up the blanket again and saw something in the corner. 'Happy Kingdom Church.'

'Ah,' Brindley's face took on a look of understanding. 'Homeless. That church gives out blankets to them. I saw a documentary just the other night. They have churches springing up all over the place.'

Storm couldn't help feeling sorry for the boy. No wonder he'd impersonated him. A life in this dirty caravan as a cage cleaner had to be better than living on the streets. He studied the blanket, wishing he had given the boy a chance to take it with him. 'Where does this church give out these blankets?'

Brindley frowned, tapping his chin. 'In the city. Um, where was it again? I'm not sure, but it's the main homeless centre. Shouldn't take much to look it up and find it.'

Storm stopped short, almost laughing at himself. What was he thinking? That kid had almost ruined his reputation. Let him find himself another blanket. Let that church give him another one. He wasn't going to bother chasing it up.

Chapter Seventeen

Kenny and his group didn't even question Tori's altered appearance when she went back to her homeless life. Despite their acceptance, despair settled deep inside. Kenny was getting closer to having a mansion, he said, and became angry when anyone suggested he might be being played. Tori noticed the change in him. He was always on edge, waiting to be found by a hit man or caught by the police. He was obsessed with doing 'just one more job' before gaining the wealth he'd been promised.

She tried to make him see sense. 'So you're happy dealing drugs?'

He pulled his hoodie further over his head and glared at her. 'No, but it's just temporary. As soon as I finish this next job they're giving me a new one.'

She was sceptical. His eyes narrowed. 'It's true. I will be on their documentaries, showing how the church helped me go from being homeless to gainfully employed and wealthy.'

'But you'll only be wealthy because of your dealing.'

'No, the dealing is just a way to prove myself before they give me the job.'

'What job?'

He looked at her as though she was stupid. 'Helping them advertise. I'll be on their TV shows. I get to say how they changed my life. I think I have to say I believe in God now or something too.' He grinned. 'Not much in exchange for a mansion, I reckon.'

'But Kenny, weren't you supposed to get that mansion months ago?'

He looked down. 'Yeah, but stuff happened and it fell through.' His eyes brightened. 'But after Wednesday's job—it's a big one—after that, it really will be mine.'

Tori said nothing, but she feared not only for his life, but for her own. She knew there was no way Kenny would ever give up his dream, even if it meant dealing drugs. Tori had seen the effect of drugs and alcohol on her mother and she wanted no part of it. Yet she didn't know where else to go. If only the real Storm Clements had never found her.

***

Storm wandered back into his caravan and fell onto his bed. He had settled back into circus life with ease. He loved the admiration and applause as he performed. Dusty Lane hadn't been in the ring for so long that Brindley tried to give him another horse. But there was no way he would work with some other horse. Dusty Lane had been his performing partner and friend since he was a toddler. They were a team.

Absently, he picked up his television remote and fiddled with it. The public had streamed in again tonight, gazing at him with glowing eyes. So why did he feel so restless and empty? With a sigh, he threw down the remote and sat on the edge of his bed. His talent set him above other people in a way made him feel good, and yet he was lonely because it also set him apart. Even the horses no longer meant as much to him. He had a desire for people; for deep relationships, love and security, and he wasn't finding it there. With a grimace he remembered the girl who had tried to catch his attention tonight, giggling and carrying on. The superficial female attention was beginning to annoy rather than flatter him. Blowing out a breath, he picked up the remote again and pressed the power button. Anything to distract him and take this awful listless feeling.

He settled back on his pillows, half-heartedly watching. It was a documentary on missing persons. The one they were talking about was beautiful. A child and teenage model with big blue eyes.

'Victoria Seeth had a brilliant future ahead of her.' The television showed the girl accepting a bouquet of flowers. She appeared shy but pleased as a sash was placed across her shoulder and an audience broke into applause.

'Victoria is wanted by police in relation to an unsolved murder case. She went missing the day of the murder and hasn't been seen since. Investigations are ongoing.'

Storm leaned up on one elbow. Something was stirring in his memory. She looked like the girl he had read about in the newspaper when he was out on the roads. He frowned, trying to remember the story. Her mother claimed she had tried to protect her from being arrested, but the girl had jumped from the car, receiving severe injuries to her arms and legs. Then later, she had climbed out a motel window, and then escaped from hospital.

Storm watched the pictures flashing across the television screen, transfixed. He had definitely seen this girl somewhere before. But where? Just on the front page of the newspaper? No, she was too familiar. It had to be somewhere else.

It took three days for him to work it out, and when he did, he sat up straight, the knowledge stunning him. The 'boy' Storm, was actually Victoria Seeth! Her hair was different, those beautiful, haunted eyes were now green and troubled, and that body was scrawny, but it was definitely her. And the scar down her arm was from where she had jumped from her mother's car.

Something in her story didn't add up. It was hard to believe this attractive young girl had turned into a murdering teenager; not without good reason. Clay's revelation about Marcos' lies had hit him hard. Things weren't always as they seemed. There was what people wanted you to believe and there was the truth.

He didn't consider going to the police. He was still a circus boy at heart so they never even entered the equation. Storm wanted to find this girl and learn what was truly going on before it was too late. The only place he could think to look was the homeless shelter in the city. It was a good place to start, anyway.

'Keep yourself safe.' Brindley said as he saw him off. 'I'll look after your horse like he's my own. And remember, there's always a place for you here. Make sure you come back, hey?'

Storm grinned. 'Dusty Lane is here. As soon as I sort this out you can be sure you'll see me again.'

Brindley rolled his eyes. 'Should have known. It's not like you'll miss any of us people or anything.'

Storm didn't answer, but for the first time he acknowledged he would. He'd have to be careful or he'd let too many people work their way into his heart. That was a dangerous thing to do.

***

Tori kept away from homeless shelters as much as possible, especially now Kenny had led them all into danger. Another group of drug dealers had threatened him, saying he was stepping on their toes, dealing to their clients in the shelter.

'I'll wait outside,' Tori told the group as they made their way into the shelter, everyone on alert. They wouldn't have come at all except that Kenny needed to connect with the church group again.

The more she thought about it, the more the idea disgusted her. Churches were supposed to help people, not get involved in crime and use homeless people for their own gains. She glanced down at the backpack at her feet and tried to quash her feelings of guilt. She had stolen it and the torch, batteries, blanket and water bottle inside from a nearby Salvation Army store that morning. She figured they would have given them to her anyway, if they'd known her need. But still, stealing bothered her.

She sat on a brick ledge outside the centre, every sense on guard. She felt, rather than saw someone approach. She stiffened and grabbed her backpack protectively, ready to run. But this man was no underworld figure. She recognised him immediately. Storm Clements.

She glanced into his dark, intense eyes and then away. 'What more do you want from me?'

When he didn't answer, her muscles tensed ready for flight, but his voice stopped her. 'So you're a girl.'

She looked up quickly. His expression was amused, if anything, though his tone was still gruff.

He casually moved toward her. She found herself involuntarily backing away.

'You're tough for a girl.' He stopped and slowly sat on the ledge beside her. 'Probably too tough.'

Tori stopped too, staring back, eyes wide. 'What are you talking about?'

'You. And your mother and that girl you're supposed to have killed.'

Fear coursed through her and she would have run, but she was caught in a rush of pounding feet coming from the shelter. It was Kenny and the gang, and in tow were men Tori instinctively knew were to be feared.

'Quick! Run!' Kenny yelled at her. Tori could have hit him. Those men wouldn't have known she was involved with the group if he hadn't called to her. Now she *had* to run!

Gun shots sounded and she was aware of Storm running just ahead of her. He was fast. They had a chance to escape. Another shot sounded and he froze. His stunned look stopped her. Had he been shot? He didn't deserve to be caught up in this. Then she saw the man ahead of him, pointing a gun directly between his eyes. And to the left was Kenny, also cornered by another man with a gun.

'What do you want?' Kenny demanded of the man before

him. Tori couldn't believe his fearlessness. He must be high on drugs again.

'Don't play stupid!' the man growled. 'We know you've been dealing on our turf. Now we're going to teach you a lesson.'

Kenny's chest puffed out. 'Do it then, but let those two go. They're not part of it.'

Tori caught her breath and waited.

'Let them go and I'll tell you everything I know.' Kenny stood like a noble hero, negotiating for her life. The men looked uncertain, until sirens blared in the distance, coming closer by the second.

The men sprang into action. 'Quick. To the truck.' They shoved Kenny, Tori and Storm toward a nearby truck and pushed them into the back, closing the door.

It was pitch black inside. Tori pulled off her backpack and felt around inside till her hands landed on her torch. Relief filled her as its strong light overcame the darkness.

Kenny had propped himself up against the side wall, and was giving Storm an apologetic look. 'Sorry, mate. It's not you they want.'

Tori studied Storm in the torch light as the truck raced through city streets and felt deep remorse that she had led him in to this. She had nothing to live for, but this young man did. For that reason alone she would fight for their lives. She watched as he took his phone from his pocket, shook his head in frustration and put it back. No signal. Maybe the metal walls of the truck were interfering? Quietly, she went to the back door and studied it. She had been locked in many places by her mother during her young life and had had plenty of time to study locks and latches. This one would be easy.

She looked back at Kenny and Storm. 'Are you guys prepared to jump?'

'Are you kidding?' Kenny shook his head. 'We'll be killed for sure at this speed. I'd prefer to risk facing these guys.'

'Not now. As soon as we slow down. They're not going to

deal with us in the middle of the city streets or out on the highway. I reckon they'll go some place isolated and they'll slow down once we're off the main road and on some rough bush track or farm road. That's when we jump.'

'What if they see us?'

Tori shook her head at Kenny's hesitation. 'What if they don't? It's dark out there, remember? And I'd prefer to have a chance to run than see them face to face and have them point that gun at our heads again.'

'Nup. Not doing it.'

'But Kenny, you're the one they're upset with.'

He shrugged. 'Not doing it.'

She turned to Storm. He hadn't spoken a word since they were captured, but now his dark eyes were searching hers, shining in the torch light. She saw hope reflected there. She wouldn't let this man die. He didn't deserve to.

She shone the torch on the door and began working. It opened and she stumbled back, quickly switching off the torch. Moonlight revealed trees whipping past them at an alarming speed. Kenny was right. They would be killed unless the truck slowed down.

The bushland grew thicker and she felt rather than heard Storm come to her side. His deep voice came in her ear.

'There is a way to jump and land that minimises injury.'

Her eyes darted to his and he shrugged. 'I've been jumping off moving horses for years. I was taught how to do it if the horse gets a fright and takes off.'

'Do you think we have time for you to teach me?'

One side of his mouth turned up in a sardonic smile. 'Are you a fast learner when your life depends on it?'

She nodded.

He pointed to the side of the road. 'Jump at that angle. Aim for a piece of soft looking grass, but make sure you time your jump to land between the trees. Try to calculate how fast we are going.'

Tori was doubtful. There were way too many trees. 'How am I supposed to calculate how fast we're going?'

He looked uncertain, then studied the road behind them. 'Yeah, that's a bit harder when you haven't had practice.'

The track became rougher and the truck slowed as grass began to show between the wheel tracks.

'Can't we just jump on there?' She pointed to the grass between the wheel tracks.

Storm bit his lip, seeming to consider. 'It might be safer. But you would have to lie there completely still until they turn a corner. Otherwise they might see you.'

She nodded and he continued his instructions. 'As you jump, curl yourself into a ball, tucking you knees under your chin and putting your arms around them, close to your body. That will help you roll. Aim to hit the ground with your shoulder first. It's better than hitting it with your head.'

Tori drew in a deep breath and put her backpack on again, shoving the torch inside. Storm stepped in front of her. 'I'll go first. Watch how I do it, then come straight after me. That way we won't be too far apart and I can find you again.'

She heard Kenny's whispered, 'You two are crazy,' just before Storm jumped.

Immediately she followed, trying to copy what she had seen him do. Her heart pounded in the moments she was in the air, then came the slam of the ground against her shoulder. At least she'd aimed in the right place. She felt herself rolling before coming to a sudden stop. Storm had told her to lie still, but she couldn't have moved if she wanted to. All the air had been knocked out of her and her body hurt, she wasn't sure where yet. Maybe everywhere.

She looked at the stars high above her for a moment. They seemed to be spinning. She closed her eyes and when she opened them again, Storm was there, leaning over her. He had his shirt off and was holding it against a gash on his shoulder.

'Landed on a stupid rock,' he said. 'What about you?'

She tried to sit up and winced. He looked amused. 'Come on, I know you're tough. And you're not bleeding as far as I can tell.'

She glared at him. It was alright for him to say. He couldn't feel all the places that would come out in decent bruises. But she knew they needed to get off the road and into the cover of the bush.

She tried to stand, but the moment she put weight on her ankle she knew she'd done some damage.

Storm was studying it, all amusement gone. His brow furrowed in concern. 'We need to keep moving. Can you walk?'

She could limp at least. She went to move forward, but gasped as he shoved his blood-soaked shirt into her hands, scooped her up and headed into the bush.

Dizziness overwhelmed her. She wasn't sure if it was the pain, the shock, or the fact that she was being held against this man's bare chest and carried through the bush in the moonlight. She studied his strong arms, then realised what she was doing and looked away, pushing against the hard muscles of his chest.

'I'll be okay now. Put me down.'

He ignored her and kept going.

She tried again. 'Your shoulder's bleeding.'

'Then hold that shirt against it for me.'

She lifted the shirt in her hands and reached up to hold it against his shoulder. 'You could have just left me, you know.'

He glanced down at her, and his eyes were hard. 'What, and never solve the famous Victoria Seeth mystery? I don't think so.'

Chapter Eighteen

'My name is not Victoria.' She seemed to spit the name. Storm lowered her to the ground. She wasn't heavy in her emaciated state, but he had to admit he was getting tired and his shoulder throbbed. He doubted it would need stitches, but it needed a rest if it was going to heal.

He pulled out his phone and cursed. Still no signal. They would probably have to climb a hill to get one. It would have to wait until morning so the girl could rest her ankle. He looked at her. She was searching through her backpack and came out with a bottle of water. She was homeless so he doubted she had food, but at least she had water.

'What's your name then?'

She shrugged. 'Call me Tori.' She took a sip of her drink. Then another.

'You might want to ration that a bit.'

'Why?' Rebellion passed through her hard green eyes.

'Because my phone has no signal so I have no idea where we are or how to get out of here. We might get a bit hungry and thirsty.'

She shrugged and he frowned. Did she truly not care? Anyone would believe she wasn't worried whether she lived or died. Well, he was.

Thankfully his time in the circus had given him opportunity to learn about the Australian bush. He had watched some of the men choose which berries and grasses to eat, and had learned to build a fire with nothing but sticks and dry leaves.

He set to work on a fire, wondering if she ever instigated conversation. Some girls talked non-stop and they annoyed him. Right now he thought the silence was worse. Her stony, watchful gaze put him on edge. What if she decided to murder him too?

He put the thought out of his mind. She was too skinny to be any kind of threat to him. She was also injured. And did he really believe she'd killed that other girl anyway?

The sticks began to smoke. He pushed some dry grass beneath them. A spark came and he looked up at her in triumph. She still studied him warily, her injured ankle now stretched out in front of her, resting on her backpack. At least she knew about rest and elevation. He wished he had some ice for her.

The fire crackled to life and he breathed a sigh of relief and sat back. He had a lot of questions for Victoria Seeth, and now was as good a time as any to ask them. 'Did you murder that girl?'

At first he thought she was going to ignore him but her indignation seemed stronger than her willpower. Her head jerked up. 'She was like a sister to me. I would never kill her.'

'That's what the media says.'

Tori shook her head. 'That's what my mother says.'

Storm started at the bitterness he heard in her voice. For a moment he thought she might be capable of murder. 'You hate your mother, don't you?'

At his question, it was as though she had suddenly been wiped of all expression. She looked cold and hard. 'She killed my sister and tried to blame me for it.'

Storm stared at her. Light from the fire danced across her face. 'How can you be so calm about something so horrible?'

She looked down and drew lines in the dirt with a stick. 'Life is horror. We're all in a fight for survival and we only have enough power to protect ourselves.'

'Has your life really been that bad?'

She looked up and her eyes challenged him but her voice was dull. 'Often I think it would be easier to just take my own life, then I could stop running. But I'm not game, because what if the afterlife is the same? What if I will just be running forever?'

Running for eternity? Storm had never heard that theory before. The only theory he had ever heard was his brother's—that you had to trust and believe in God and the afterlife would be perfect. Otherwise it would be awful. He'd never believed it himself, but here was someone who needed some kind of hope—a hope like Prince's. She needed a rainbow to cling to through the storm, as Prince had put it. He still didn't understand anything, except that this girl had been through more than he could ever imagine. And now he had been forced to go through some of it with her.

'So why are you running?'

She gave a mirthless laugh, looking down at her ankle. 'Not running now, am I?'

He wasn't going to let her avoid the question. 'You would be if you could. And I think you owe me some kind of explanation. After all, you got me into this mess.'

'I didn't ask you to follow me.' She glared at him and he smiled. He wasn't intimidated by a few nasty looks. He was an expert at them himself. '

He studied her as she continued to draw in the dirt. Finally, she met his gaze. 'Will you leave me alone if I tell you?'

'If you tell me the truth, yes.'

'How will you know?'

He steadily met her gaze. 'I'll know.'

She considered him a moment before looking somewhere into the distance. 'It's not a pretty story.'

'I figured that.' He gave a laugh that didn't come out properly.

Her clear green eyes penetrated his before she sighed. His eyes never leaving her, Storm sat across from her, waiting. With a deep breath, she began her story.

As Storm listened to her describe her childhood, travelling from one modelling appointment, competition or audition to another and of her mother's obsession and passion. He felt his heart go out to this ragged, skinny girl.

When she explained about the way her mother treated Sarah, and the day she'd been taken from school and told of her death, Storm watched for emotion in her, but there was none. It was as though she was detached from all she was describing.

She didn't look at Storm until she confessed to living in his caravan. Her eyes darted away and back again as though expecting to see the anger he'd first shown.

Her eyebrows rose in surprise. 'No comment?'

His gaze didn't leave hers. 'Go on. I'm listening.'

She narrowed her eyes. 'And doubting.'

'No. I believe you.'

She let out a breath and relief relaxed her features for a moment. When she finished her story, she sat silently, waiting for a response.

For a long time he didn't speak. Her story cut him inside, and yet she sat there impassively. It wasn't normal.

He frowned. 'Don't you have any emotions at all?' He poked a stick in the fire, encouraging its warmth. 'If I had been through what you have been through, I'd be a mess, but you're sitting here without even shedding a tear as though none of this has affected you at all.'

Tori licked her lips. 'Maybe I don't know how to cry. Maybe I'm past being human.'

He thought he understood. Everything she had was going into her survival. He'd never been one for compassion or understanding, and so the feeling that filled him now left him in shock. Here was someone who was far from weak, and yet who was vulnerable. She fought long and hard, yet still she was losing every battle she ever fought. It didn't seem fair.

'You can't live out here forever. You have to give yourself up. They'll believe you.'

Tori shook her head. 'You don't know my mother. Why do you think she got away with the way she treated Sarah and me for so long? We had plenty of welfare workers come to our home to check us out, but they always left again, believing her stories.'

'So what are you going to do?'

'Escape. Again. Leave this hopeless existence behind.'

A sinking feeling filled his gut. 'What do you mean?'

She shrugged and averted her gaze, staring at the ground in silence. She couldn't mean she would take her own life, surely? She wouldn't do that, would she?

CHAPTER NINETEEN

After several hours, it became apparent that Storm wasn't planning to leave her alone; not until he convinced her to give herself up to the authorities. Tomorrow he was going to take them to the top of a hill so they could get a signal on his phone, he said, then his phone navigator would get them out of the bush. He was as determined as she was and she didn't want to fight any longer.

Slowly, she stood. His head jerked up and his dark eyes scrutinised her. 'Where are you going?'

'I need the toilet. Or a tree. Or whatever I can find out here.'

He searched her eyes, then seeming satisfied, watched her limp a few metres away. She was surprised at how calm she felt as she deliberately walked behind a tree so he couldn't see her any more. Then, as quietly as she could, she limped her way to the cliff edge she'd noticed earlier when Storm was carrying her. There was no fear, just resignation. She refused to think beyond the chance to sink into nothingness. If there was an afterlife, surely she could have a bit of sleep before she was plunged into it and all it entailed.

***

Storm couldn't believe what he was seeing. Something had urged him to follow Tori when she moved out of sight. He could now see her standing on the edge of a cliff, focussing on the ground far below. There was no way he could get to her in time if she chose to jump. Her foot moved forward and a stone dislodged. He heard it bounce a few times until the sound faded away.

'Don't do it, Tori!' His voice echoed through the night air and she turned.

'I can't lose my freedom, Storm.'

He edged closer. 'Who says you will?'

'I'm tired, Storm.' She returned her gaze to the gaping chasm in front of her. In her words he heard her heart. She wasn't just physically tired, she was emotionally drained and mentally exhausted. She didn't want to carry on.

'I know, but there's something I have to tell you before you die.' He tried to remain calm, but his voice was urgent. At first she didn't respond and he sighed, knowing he had just been clutching at straws.

'It will change your life—give you hope.' His voice, now calm, belied the way his heart was hammering in fear.

She stepped back, her attention caught, and Storm darted forward with lightning reflexes and grabbed her, pulling her away from the edge. He'd been prepared for the way she would fight and used all the strength he had to hold her. Although tired, she seemed to muster energy from somewhere and it took a while for her to finally stop in his arms.

'You were lying,' she said, and he could hear the desperation and anger in her voice. 'I should have known! How stupid am I? Everyone has lied to me all my life and I chose to believe you.'

'I wasn't lying. I have something to tell you.'

Still she didn't relax and Storm knew that if he let her go she wouldn't give him another chance to stop her jumping off that cliff. And so, every sense alert, he began to speak in a low voice into her ear so close to his. 'My family knows about the afterlife.'

She was staring at the ground so he turned her slightly to meet her eyes. The clear green was filled with pain. He had to convince her. 'My oldest brother is a minister and claims he talks to God. My next brother helps out with the homeless. They've been through a lot, but they haven't had to harden their hearts like you have. Like I have. I think it's because of God.'

He didn't know if Tori was listening, but he needed to hear the words himself.

'I haven't ever listened to what they believed because I guess I thought I had plenty of time on earth and that life isn't that bad. But after meeting you, I know it can be and I want to find out more about this God thing for you so you can have a better life.'

Still Tori said nothing.

'Sometimes you have to cling to rainbows, Victoria.'

'Tori.' It was whispered, but he heard it.

'Sometimes you have to cling to rainbows, Tori, because they're a sign of hope and beauty after the storm. They show that even though it's raining the sun will come out. It might feel like some storms will last forever, but none do. Not really. That's what my brother says, anyway.'

***

Tori sighed. She had given up believing there could be any 'sunlight' in her life, as Storm had put it.

But he looked so earnest. Then she noticed his shoulder.

'You're bleeding again.'

He glanced at the trickle of blood and shrugged. 'Yeah, well, you fought me pretty hard.'

'Where's your shirt?'

'Back there at the fire.'

She frowned. 'Won't the fire lead them to us?'

He quirked an eyebrow. 'You're thinking of the future again. That's good. And no, I don't think they'll bother with us. They were just out to scare us. It worked, didn't it?'

She didn't answer but tried to pull away from him. He didn't let her. Instead, he pulled her back toward the campfire,

144

supporting her as she limped. His vice-like grip on her wrist hurt, but she didn't complain. It meant she didn't have to decide to run, because she couldn't.

The fire was dying down. Still holding her hand, he kicked around some grass and leaves to soften the ground for them. 'Get some sleep.' His order was gruff and she turned to stare at him. He could order her around all he liked, but the moment he was asleep the urge to disappear would return, along with the emptiness and weariness. Maybe he could sleep, but she certainly couldn't.

Storm studied her and seemed to read her thoughts, then he gently pushed her down. He lay close beside her, his arm across her back. It wasn't firm, but Tori knew the moment she moved it would be. He wasn't going to let her go anywhere. For some reason, he cared that she lived.

There was comfort in his warm hand on her back. Her mind was still foggy and refused to settle. Eventually, hunger and exhaustion left her with the inability to think or plan any longer. As she lay there, a vision of a rainbow came to her mind and in moments, she was fast asleep.

***

Storm sighed with relief at her steady breathing, but couldn't bring himself to sleep. Apart from the discomfort of sleeping on the ground, his thoughts were consumed with all he'd been through that day. He'd never been so aware of death. Hopelessness had never been so real.

They needed to see his brother. Tori needed to hear the message of hope and find a way to live. True, she wouldn't agree to it unless she kept her identity a secret. He could get in trouble for protecting her, but it couldn't be worse than Tori being out here alone in the bush, working out ways to take her own life.

He awoke the moment she moved. She was staring at him, those clear green eyes close to his. He lifted his head and allowed her to move slightly. She rubbed her eyes and blinked, looking around. To his relief, she looked refreshed.

'We'll find somewhere we can get a signal and then go to my brother's today.'

'I'm not giving myself up, Storm.'

He nodded. 'I'm not asking you to. We won't go to Blaze's place – he's a minister so I think he would legally have to give you up; it's called mandatory reporting or something. We'll go to my other brother's place.'

Tori studied him for a moment, seeming to ascertain his trustworthiness. 'I don't want to be in jail where I can't make any choices for myself.'

'What, like taking your life?' She didn't answer and he knew he'd hit the nail on the head.

'So are you coming?' He stood and reached a hand to her. She hesitated, then took it. Her hand seemed so small and thin in his.

He smiled and squeezed it. His deep voice came out soft. 'You can trust me. I promise.'

Chapter Twenty

Tori kept a close eye on Storm as they made their way up a hill. Her ankle was still tender but improved enough to bear her weight. Breathing hard, she stopped to rest, lowering herself onto a rock. Storm sat beside her. His blood-stained shirt now hung over one shoulder and she was grateful to see the gash was no longer bleeding. It was clear his brown skin was used to seeing the sun.

She pulled her water bottle out of her back pack and took a long sip before offering it to Storm. He nodded his thanks and gulped a mouthful before handing it back and checking his phone. He smiled. 'We've got signal.'

'Already?'

'Yep. Must be a phone tower not too far away. That's hopeful.' He swiped his thumb across the screen a few times. His dark eyes lit up. 'And here we are.' He shoved his phone in front of her. She squinted, trying to make out the map with the bright sun reflecting off the screen. He jabbed his finger at a red dot.

'That's us.' He moved the screen along and pointed to a yellow line. 'And that's a road. We'll head that way and call my brother to come and get us.'

She nodded, but couldn't believe it was quite that easy. Something would stop them for sure. His phone charge would run out, or the men would decide to come back and get them, or one of them would get injured, or they would run out of food and water before they reached their destination.

Or was God really helping them? She tried to push down the glimmer of hope building up within her. She thought it had died along with Sarah and had felt safer that way.

Storm was speaking again. 'We'll go around this way so we can get water.' He pointed to his phone. 'There's a creek there we can follow for a bit. And I'll show you what we can eat along the way.'

He sounded so confident she wondered if anyone ever dared question him. He had a commanding presence that made her feel safe. She might as well trust him. What did she have to lose?

***

The bush cleared and the sound of cars wafted through the air. Storm let out a cheer and threw his arms around Tori. To his surprise, sweaty as they both were, she hugged him back.

'Prince should be here any minute.'

She stiffened. 'Prince?'

'Yeah, my brother. I called him a couple of hours ago, remember? He said he'd meet us here and take us back to his place.' He studied her, noticing how pale she'd become. He'd kept her eating and drinking but she didn't look good.

God, I don't even believe in you, but she needs you and she needs help soon.

A car slowed on the busy highway and Storm chuckled. 'Here he is now. Can you believe it?' She didn't answer and he wondered if he really believed it himself. The previous twenty-four hours were starting to feel like some crazy dream.

Prince jumped out, engine still running, and came to him. 'Storm! What's going on? Are you crazy? What are you doing stuck out here in the middle of nowhere? Rachel's worried sick about you. You could have at least told me what was happening.'

'Couldn't. My phone was running low. Let's get in the car.'

He herded Tori into the car, surprised at the way she kept

her head down as though trying to hide her face. What was up with her now? He tried to catch her gaze but she didn't give him a chance. She looked as though she hadn't washed or eaten for months. She needed a good shower and a sleep.

'So what's the go?' Prince pulled his door shut and pulled out onto the road, building up speed.

Storm bit his lip. 'Can it wait until we get to your place?'

'I don't know. Can it?'

Storm glanced to where Tori sat huddled in the back. 'I think it needs to. I'm not even sure what to tell you.'

Prince glanced at him. 'How about the truth?'

Storm grunted. How much of the truth was safe to tell? He wasn't sure, but he had a bit of time to work it out.

'Did you bring something to eat?'

Prince gave him a look. 'Yeah. Just like you ordered. But I only had time to grab a loaf of bread.'

Storm glanced into the back seat to see it and grabbed it, passing a few pieces to Tori. Bread had never tasted so good.

***

Tori woke refreshed but still tense. The knot in her stomach tightened as she realised what had woken her. Prince had turned off the engine and glanced back. 'We're here.'

Her heart thundered in her chest. Why hadn't she seen the similarities between Storm and the man who'd stopped her stealing the blanket at the homeless shelter? It was so obvious, now they both sat in front of her. How ironic that she had escaped drug dealers just to land right back in a car with another.

Or was he? Had he known what the church was doing? She would have to tread carefully.

'You ready?' Storm asked quietly. Tori simply nodded while he led her to the door.

A young blonde haired woman with a sweet smile opened

it. She gave a delighted cry and threw her arms around Storm, then looked to her.

Storm pulled her forward. 'Rachel, this is Tori.'

Rachel smiled, though she looked a little flustered. No doubt she had never seen such a grotty girl looking like a boy before.

'Come in,' she said, before moving past them and putting her arms around Prince's neck. He hugged her close and kissed her, subtly shaking his head. 'No answers yet. Storm wanted to wait till we got home.'

Tori knew they deserved an explanation, but she wasn't ready to give herself up. They didn't understand what her mother was like. Nothing was worth the risk of being sent back to live with her again. It would be better to die.

She was vaguely aware of Storm leading her to a lounge chair. The cushions sank as he sat beside her.

'We need somewhere to stay for a while,' Storm said without preamble. Both Rachel and Prince gave him their full attention.

'For how long?'

Storm shrugged. 'I've no idea. As long as you'll have us, I guess. Don't worry, I'll find work and pay for our keep.'

'Okay, but you're not staying in the same room.'

Storm's eyes narrowed but his brother's matched his.

'I'm not naive, Storm. We come from the circus, remember? I've seen plenty of girls performing as boys. We don't need secrets in this house. So what's the story?'

'Story?'

'Yes. You know we'll love and accept her. We won't judge.'

It was then it hit Tori. Prince thought she was pregnant with Storm's child. Storm seemed to realise it at the same time. He jumped up, eyes blazing with anger.

'You think she's pregnant? How dare you, Prince!' He gritted his teeth, dark eyes blazing. 'I'm not like you! I learned from your stupid mistakes. I've done nothing to Tori except protect her and try to help her find a reason to live.' He turned to her. 'Come on, let's go.'

Tori began to stand, but Prince held Storm back.

'Wait!' he commanded. 'I'm sorry, okay?'

Storm's eyes were still blazing, but he slowly sat back down, taking Tori's hand so that she did the same. He sat erect, still tense with anger.

'So tell me what's really going on,' Prince said.

'I can't.'

Rachel cut in, her warm gaze settling on her and making her feel loved and accepted for no reason. 'Your real name is Tori?'

When she didn't answer, Prince shook his head, looking at Storm. 'I want to help, but I can't have someone staying in my house without knowing why they're here and a little bit about them. How do I know she's not dealing drugs or running from the law or something?'

Tori gasped, pain searing through her heart. This man, who supposedly was going to give her hope, was actually a drug dealer. It appeared he knew all about the Happy Kingdom Church and their purpose in 'helping' the homeless. She jumped to her feet.

'You won't let me stay here if I deal drugs?' She almost snorted. Her mother would have been horrified. Beauty queens didn't snort. She pointed a shaking finger at Prince, her voice growing louder until she was screaming at him. 'You hypocrite. I don't understand how you can go about pretending to do God's work, being part of a church that is so ... so ... ' She sputtered to a stop. She shouldn't have dared hope. She shouldn't have trusted Storm. Emotional pain so strong it became physical curled around her. Sobs broke out, building up from somewhere deep inside. Now she'd begun to release the anguish she had no strength to stop it in all its force. A vision of Sarah flashed through her mind until she collapsed into someone's arms.

'Tori. Tori.' For a long time she had heard nothing but

the buzzing in her ears. She was so tired, so weak and hungry. But now she heard a deep, gentle voice coaxing her back into reality. And there was a baby crying somewhere in the background. Had her yelling woken a baby? What did she care? No doubt she was about to be killed for exposing Storm's brother, Prince, the drug dealer.

But it was Prince who was calling her name, leaning over the chair she lay in, looking like he actually cared. And Rachel was right by his side, her eyes wide and frightened. But it didn't look like she feared for herself. If she didn't know better she would think Rachel was afraid for *her.*

Prince was studying her intently. 'Tori, I don't work for the church any more. We had some differences and I left. But what do you mean about them being drug dealers?'

She tried to speak but her voice came out raspy. 'In the blankets. They put the drugs in the blankets. The blanket I took that day was meant for Kenny.'

'What blanket? Who is Kenny?'

'That lady yelled for you to stop me. I took the blanket meant for Kenny.'

Prince's eyes widened with sudden recognition. 'You're the girl I stopped that night?'

Tori didn't answer as she studied Prince and Rachel. They certainly weren't acting like drug dealers. They looked confused. Did she dare tell them?

Her eyes darted to the doorway. Storm stood there, a baby in his arms. The baby reached for his face, and chuckling, Storm moved his head out of the way. Did drug dealers have children? She supposed they did. But did they look so warm and caring?

Storm stepped forward. 'You can trust them, Tori.'

She had to believe eyes that looked at her that way. Slowly, she sat up. 'They gave out mints in the blankets. Only they weren't mints.'

She saw a look pass between Prince and Rachel. It was one of stunned recognition.

'What did they look like?'

'They were individually wrapped in small white plastic wrappers.'

Prince moved back and sank into the lounge opposite her. Rachel stood. 'Prince, do you have any here?'

He shook his head.

Tori's brows rose. 'You've had one?'

'Several. They give them out at the Happy Kingdom Church.'

Tori licked her lips, suddenly aware how dry they were. 'Did anything ever happen?'

Prince began to shake his head, then stopped, swallowing hard. He looked at Rachel. 'Well, I guess I … I blacked out once. And I felt like I was on a high …' His voice faded out.

'They're drugs?' Rachel's look was incredulous and her voice came out in a kind of squeak.

Tori nodded. 'That's why that lady was so upset when I took that blanket meant for Kenny. He's a dealer.'

Prince paled and his hands were shaking. He glanced at Rachel. 'It seemed strange at the time. I thought Deborah was over-reacting, but if she was protecting drugs …'

Rachel looked around the room as though searching for solid ground. Nobody spoke for a time. Finally, Prince reached for the phone. 'I need to call the police.'

Terror filled Tori and she jumped up, grabbing his arm. 'No. Please, you can't!'

'Tori, they're drug dealers.'

Storm stepped forward. His voice was calm and commanding. 'Don't call the police, Prince. We have to find another way around this.'

Prince frowned. 'I can't *not* call the police. You know that, Storm.'

Storm stood his ground. 'There's a lot more to this than you know. I need you to trust me. If I tell you, it could put you and Rachel in danger, but if you just let Tori stay here without questioning, you'll be safe.'

Prince's eyes narrowed into a challenge. 'You've brought danger into my home?'

Storm shook his head. 'I would never do that. Sounds to me like you've done it well enough yourself, with that Happy Kingdom Church.'

The tension in the room heightened until Tori squeezed her eyes shut and took a deep breath.

'Storm, we have to tell them.'

His eyes questioned her and she nodded. There was nothing else left to do but tell her full story. And so quietly, his hand still on Tori's, Storm began. She liked his voice when it wasn't gruff or commanding. It was deep, calm and expressive. He relayed to Prince and Rachel all she had told him. He relayed it almost word for word, and Tori focused on his face. He cared. Why, she had no idea.

When Storm told them the way he'd found her standing at the cliff edge she dared sneak a peek at Prince and Rachel. What she saw shook her to the core. Rachel's brown eyes were streaming with tears and her sweet face was crumpled as she held in silent sobs. Her eyes slid shut before she moved forward and threw her arms around Tori.

It reminded her of Sarah, and for just a moment, she struggled with emotions she'd put aside a long time ago. But she pushed them away again before they could overwhelm her.

***

'I think you need to hand yourself in to the police so the truth can come out.'

Prince sounded so sure of himself that Storm wondered if he

would force Tori to do just that. He saw the way she flinched and hoped she wouldn't run. Prince needed to tread carefully.

Rachel moved to Tori and put a protective arm around her. 'I think first she needs a meal, a shower and some clean clothes. And a place to sleep. She's not going anywhere, are you Tori? No one's in immediate danger so we can wait and pray.'

Storm glanced to the room Kylie had been sleeping in. What would she think about all this? Rachel seemed to read his thoughts.

'Kylie's gone.'

'Why?'

Rachel's smile was serene. 'God had done all he needed to do with her here. And obviously, he knew Tori was coming.'

Storm wanted to give his normal condescending response to that comment, but he found it stuck in his throat. He was here to convince Tori that life had meaning. He'd better start acting like it was true if he wanted her to believe it.

When Tori emerged from the shower, clean and well-dressed despite the clothes being too large for her, Storm smiled, trying not to stare.

She looked totally different. She looked female. Her eyes were greener and her eyelashes longer. Her hair, though clean, was still knotted, but for the first time, he saw the beautiful model he'd seen in the newspaper and on the documentary. Even her lips looked a darker shade of red.

He shook his head to dispel the thought and turned his attention to Seton and Blythe, who now lay on their stomachs on the floor.

'I want you to meet my niece and nephew.' He heard the pride in his own voice and wondered what was happening to him. He sounded downright soppy. He couldn't let it be!

'This is Seton and this is Blythe.' He pointed to each in an off-handed way while Blythe looked up and gave him a wide, dimpled smile. What did she have to do that? Now he had to smile back. She giggled and he couldn't help himself. He bent down and picked her up. Her slobbery hand slid down his face and he knew he should be disgusted. Instead, he grinned at her and prepared to hand her to Tori.

She backed away, arms crossed. 'No, thanks.'

Storm smiled, not put off by her tone. 'Come on, they don't bite. They don't even have any teeth.'

Tori stared at him, then down into the little face Storm held so close to hers. The baby was smiling up at her. Storm smiled at her too, a challenge in his eyes.

Tori uncrossed her arms and allowed him to place Blythe in them. The little face screwed up. She let out wail and Tori shoved her back into his arms.

'All you have to do is smile and talk to her,' Storm said, putting Blythe up over his shoulder. Immediately, she stopped crying.

Tori stared at him. He realised then he'd never seen her smile. Did she even know how?

'I'm not good with babies,' she said. 'I'm going to have a rest.'

With that, she went to the room with the bed Rachel had made up for her and shut the door.

He let her go. She was exhausted. She would probably fall asleep the moment her head hit the pillow, if only she would trust she was safe. Blythe let out a giggle in his arms and he put a finger to the baby's lips. 'Sh, little one. She needs a lot of rest. Maybe then she'll be able to smile again.'

He went out to find Rachel in the lounge room with Seton.

'So where'd your cousin Kylie go?'

Rachel smiled. 'She's gone to stay with Grandma and Grandpa for a while. She's going to help them out with Paul until we're able to have him here.'

'Your little brother?' Storm asked in surprise.

Rachel nodded.

Storm chuckled. 'I never imagined Kylie to be the sort of person who would take to kids.'

Rachel's mouth turned up at the corners and she put a hand across it to try to hide her smile. Storm pretended to glare.

'What?' he demanded, looking down at the baby in his arms. 'Just because I hold them to help you out sometimes doesn't mean I've taken to them.'

Rachel held out her hands in mock defence and took a step back. 'I wouldn't dare suggest such a thing!'

Storm grinned, but as he looked down at Blythe resting so peacefully in his arms, he wondered how anyone could hurt a child. How could Victoria Seeth's mother have treated her so appallingly? Blythe wasn't even his own, but the fierce protectiveness he felt for her surprised him.

CHAPTER TWENTY-ONE

Tori didn't wake until the sun shone through the blinds from high in the sky, making patterns across her bed. She had no idea what the day would bring, but she was desperate to find out about Prince and Rachel's God.

Disappointment filled her when she realised Storm had forgotten his promise. The moment she was up he called in Prince and Rachel and they sat at the table while she ate breakfast, trying to convince her to go to the police and expose her mother as the murderer she was.

'We've looked up all about it on the internet this morning,' Storm told her. 'They already have suspicions about your mum. They just don't have enough evidence. She's already in custody.'

'Police are trained to spot inconsistencies.' Prince joined his brother's case. 'Justice will be served.'

Tori narrowed her eyes at Storm. 'You promised me …'

Storm nodded. 'I know, I said we wouldn't force you, and we won't, but the truth can't come out unless you tell it.'

She threw down the spoon she held in her hand and it made a loud clatter against her cereal bowl. She shoved it aside and glared at Storm. He didn't even know what promise she was talking about. All he could think about was putting her mother in jail. What about eternity? What about hope for her?

'Truth, Storm?' Everyone was staring at her in shock as she

banged her fist on the table. 'You promised me truth if I came here, remember? You promised I would find a reason to live and hope for the future. You promised I would find out about the afterlife.'

Silence followed for a full minute. Finally Prince cleared his throat. 'I can tell you, if you want to know.'

Tori felt calm steal over her. 'Now?'

Prince nodded. 'It's simple. God planned you even before you were born. He loves you, but like every single human you ignored him and didn't believe in him and lived life your own way.'

'But I didn't even know about him.'

'Did you ever look at the world around you and realise there had to be more? Did you ever have religious education classes at school, or know a Christian? Did you suspect there might be a God, but not try to find out more?'

Tori didn't answer, but his words struck a chord. Patrick was a Christian. And God had placed a Bible in her room at the motel. And that lady, Cheryl, gave her a lift to the circus and told her Jesus loved her. Did God arrange all that for her?

Prince glanced at Rachel, and she nodded for him to go on. 'Not listening to that something deep inside that tells us there is a God because we want to do things our own way means we don't deserve to go to be with him when we die. Our selfishness and living for ourselves, for our own happiness, is sin.'

Tori nodded. Maybe she wasn't as violent and abusive as her mother, but she had lived for herself her whole life.

Prince was speaking again. 'God wanted a relationship with us so badly that he sent his son, Jesus, to earth as a human so we could relate to him. Jesus died in our place, then rose back to life again to prove he is God and that what he did was enough. So if we believe in him we can know God again, be friends with him on earth, and go to heaven to be with him when we die.'

'That's it?' Tori breathed. 'That's what you believe that makes you different?'

Prince nodded. 'That's it.'

He took his Bible from the shelf and read her the story of Jesus' death and the thief on the cross beside him.

'This thief was promised he would go to heaven and all he did was believe Jesus was God and trust him with his life.'

Tori bit her lip. Whether or not she voiced it, she believed. It had to have been God who stopped her taking her life. He had made Storm's phone keep its charge long enough to bring her here. There were so many times she could have given up, but always something … no, someone, had kept that small spark of hope alive, that she was worth much more than her physical beauty. She met Prince's gaze. 'Well, I believe. I want God to be part of my life. I want to have what you and Rachel have.'

Prince looked to Rachel. 'What do we do now?'

Rachel chuckled. 'Well, my dad had a prayer he used to get people to pray, just to confirm what has already happened in their hearts. I can't remember it but I remember the general idea.' She smiled at Tori. 'Do you want me to pray and you say Amen at the end if you agree?'

She nodded. Rachel reached for her hand and then for Prince's. Tentatively, she accepted Rachel's hand, feeling the warmth as it enclosed hers. Then she noticed Storm on her other side. His hand sat on the table, waiting. She bit her lip, then met his eyes. He almost imperceptibly winked. She grabbed his hand, averting her eyes and focussed back on Rachel. Surely he hadn't really just winked at her?

A strange feeling fluttered in her chest. Didn't he realise this was the most important moment of her life? She didn't want his playful teasing or whatever it was. She wanted to give her life to God.

Rachel began to pray. 'Lord, thank you for showing Tori that she can trust you. Thank you that she is now giving her life to you, trusting that you sent Jesus to die for her. Lord Jesus, continue to open her eyes to the truth. Thank you that you promise to now live within her heart, her closest friend, always by her side. Thank you that we are never alone. We trust you with our lives.'

Tori let out a deep sigh as the prayer finished. She had much more to learn, but she was safe. She had both a reason to live and a reason to never fear dying.

'You can have this,' Prince told her, handing her the Bible he had just read from. Tori reached for it, her heart pounding. In here were the stories that would tell her about the God she would now live with forever and live for. She looked across at Storm, but Storm didn't smile the way she expected him to. His expression was both serious and thoughtful.

***

Rachel worked a comb through Tori's matted hair as she sat in front of the dressing table mirror. And as she did, she talked. Tori listened, trying not to wince as knot by knot was pulled and untangled.

As Rachel openly shared her life and heart, it crossed Tori's mind that she connected more with Rachel than she ever had with anyone, including Sarah. Talking with Rachel was like opening a treasure chest. Her knowledge and love of God was so full and deep. Her life experiences were rich. Tori simply couldn't hear enough of what it meant to truly walk with God.

'So no matter what you do, God forgives?' Tori's studied Rachel's face in the mirror. 'I mean, sleeping with someone before you're married is a bit different from murdering someone, isn't it?'

Rachel's warm brown eyes met hers. 'No. It's all sin. It's all rebelling against God's best plan for our lives. But no matter what you've done, if you're sorry and ask him to forgive, he will.'

'So my mum ... if she was sorry ...'

'She could be forgiven.'

Tori was silent for a good many minutes as she wrestled with that. Her mother could be forgiven and change. But she wanted her mother to pay for what she had done! Yet she was aware she hadn't led a perfect life, either. There had been lies, bitterness, anger, deception, and more recently, stealing. In a strange way, Tori still loved her mother. She always would; after all, she was now the only family she had.

'If I were to give myself up, I could talk to my mum,' Tori said softly.

Rachel simply nodded.

'And if I don't, you could be in trouble for harbouring me.'

Again, Rachel nodded.

'So why are you doing this for me?'

Rachel hesitated before she came to stand directly in front of Tori. 'Not so long ago Prince and I went to a new church. Someone there said something that, well, it threw me a bit at the time.' Rachel took a deep breath. 'This person had a dream about Prince and I looking after a girl who was lost and alone in the world. She said we helped her. What if that girl she was talking about was you?'

'Huh?' Tori frowned. Rachel wasn't making sense. 'You would put your life on the line for something a stranger said to you about something supposedly happening in the future? Sounds a bit sus to me. It could cost you everything. Your freedom. Your twins.'

Rachel's eyes darkened. 'Prince and I prayed about it last night and we believe God was giving us a message that day. He was reassuring us it's okay to have you here. We love you, Tori. Jesus gave up his life for you and he hasn't yet made it clear to us that we should do anything but love you. It's up to you to do the right thing.'

But despite Tori's belief in God, there were some things in her life she couldn't let go of. Rachel talked about total surrender to God, but it was impossible. She'd battled on her own for so long she didn't know how to let go. She'd fought to protect herself from hurt all her life, and couldn't let anyone into her heart.

She watched Prince and Rachel all day; the way they showed their love for one another both in affection and selflessness. Prince washed up when Rachel was tired and Rachel changed all the dirty nappies because she said Prince found it distasteful. They openly shared their love and wore their hearts on their sleeves. Tori doubted she could ever express herself like that.

She sat in the lounge room with Storm after tea, listening to the sounds of Prince and Rachel bathing Blythe and preparing her for bed. Storm held a contented Seton in his lap but she knew he was studying her.

Suddenly he said, 'You don't look so much like a homeless street urchin anymore.'

Caught off guard, she said the first thing that came to her mind. 'And you don't look so much like a bush pig.'

His mouth dropped open, then he chuckled. 'You'll keep.'

Remorse filled her. 'Storm, I'm sorry. You've done so much for me and then I go and say something like that.'

His eyes twinkled at her. 'I don't mind. It's good to see you have a sense of humour. You might even be human. Anything's possible.'

Yes, anything was possible. She was beginning to believe that.

'You thought more about going to the police?'

She hesitated at his question, then looked down into her lap. She hated to disappoint him. 'Yes, but I'm not ready yet.'

'When will you be ready?'

She avoided his intense dark eyes, and when she remained silent, he leaned forward, removing baby Seton from his lap and lowering him gently to the rug on the floor.

'We have to face them, Tori.' His tone was firm. 'It's the only way to be free. And Rachel says she believes justice will be done. God tells her things like that.'

'I thought you didn't believe in God.'

Storm grinned. 'I don't really. But then, I must, because I made a deal with him, and you can't make deals with someone who doesn't exist.'

Tori's brows rose. 'What was the deal?'

He shrugged, lifting one leg across the other and leaning back into the lounge. 'That if all this turns out right for you I'll believe.'

Tori couldn't help letting out a sound close to a laugh. 'But you've confessed you already believe.'

Storm shrugged again, his expression sheepish. 'Maybe I'll change that to I'll follow God and be a Christian like Prince and Rachel.'

'But if God's real, shouldn't you be a Christian anyway, whether or not this all turns out right?'

***

Storm studied Tori. There was still an air of sadness about her, but there was no longer despair. He had to admit she was attractive. To begin with, he'd felt nothing but protection toward her as another human being who was suffering, but now he felt much more. He fought the feelings as best he could. And now she had challenged him and the challenge was eating into his heart and mind.

He'd tried to make a deal with God, but the truth was, he'd already come to believe. Tori also believed, but watching her, he knew there was more to it than that. Perhaps believing gave you entry into heaven, but it seemed you needed to go a step further and surrender your whole life to God if you truly wanted to change and know the joy and peace Prince and Rachel did.

He was going to commit himself to do more than believe. He would commit himself to knowing God and having a relationship with him.

I guess it starts here, God. He prayed silently but he knew God heard. *We need to talk about a lot of things. About you and me. And Tori.*

Something shifted in his heart. The self-sufficient, capable Storm Clements now knew he needed and wanted a relationship with God. He asked God to forgive him for all his selfish pride; the way he had lived for himself and cut others down to build himself up.

True, he might be able to make it on his own, but Storm wanted to live life to the full. He wanted to live the life God had always planned for him. For the first time he understood that true strength was in laying down your own life, like Jesus had done for him.

Chapter Twenty-Two

Rachel and Prince were sitting in the kitchen feeding the twins when Tori ventured out for breakfast the next morning.

'Tori. We have something to ask you.'

She stiffened, then made herself relax. She was so defensive, but she knew these people weren't out to hurt her.

'Some of our relatives haven't met the twins yet. We've arranged for them to come tomorrow for a bit of a family reunion to meet them. It's been arranged for a while. Would you be comfortable being here?'

'How would you explain who I am?'

Rachel smiled. 'You're our friend. We're helping you out for a bit and you're helping us with the twins.'

Tori nodded. 'That's fine. I'll just go to my room if—'

She jumped as the doorbell pealed. Prince stood.

'I'll get it.' He strode down the hallway to answer the door. She heard the silence that followed, and curious, peeked around the corner.

That woman stood there. The blanket woman. Another man stood by her side. She knew it must be Deborah and Parker from the Happy Kingdom Church and dread crept up her spine. What would Prince do?

'Prince, we have another proposition for you.' The man sounded confident and firm. Like a salesman.

Prince looked taken aback. Then he stood taller. 'I'm sorry, I'm not interested.'

Parker stepped forward. 'Just hear me out.'

Prince took a fortifying breath and looked behind him. He spotted Tori.

'Get Rachel,' he mouthed. 'And Storm.'

Tori nodded and raced to get them. Prince still hadn't invited the couple in and Tori knew that he wouldn't.

Rachel asked her to keep an eye on the twins while she went to join him. Storm strode to his brother's side, and looked the couple up and down. Tori stood just inside the kitchen, keeping one eye on the twins, and the other on the front door. Despite looking different from the homeless girl who'd stolen the blanket from them, she kept in the background, not wanting to be recognised.

Storm was playing his best commanding, scornful self. Rachel stood at Prince's other side, her arm tucked firmly around his waist.

'What can we do for you?' Prince asked.

Parker looked at the trio, annoyed, then back to Prince. 'This isn't necessary. What I have to say is your business. This is your choice to make.'

Prince opened his mouth to speak, but Parker rushed on. 'We want you to help us with another project. We are making a documentary about our work with the homeless. We want you to interview Kenny, our success story.'

Kenny. Tori breathed a sigh of relief. He must be alive.

Prince went to speak, but Parker held up his hand. 'You don't have to come to our church or be a member. We'll pay you well.' He shoved a glossy brochure under Prince's nose. 'We will give you this home to live in free of charge. All of you. Rachel too, of course. We promise not to mention Rachel's … uh, spiritual condition again.'

Tori tried to catch a glimpse of the brochure. From Rachel's gasp she knew it wasn't any old home that was being offered.

'Why?' Prince's question was direct.

Tori saw the way Deborah stepped forward. She wondered how the woman had managed to keep quiet this long without taking over. 'Because we have so much to offer. We believe God directed us to you to rain his blessings down upon you. Maybe this will draw you back into the fold.'

Prince said nothing and Tori waited with bated breath. Of course Prince wouldn't accept, no matter how attractive the offer, but would he mention the drug dealing? How would the couple react? Would they become violent? Would they send hit men to kill them off?

Prince looked down at the brochure, then back to the couple. 'When do I have to let you know?'

Parker glanced to Deborah and a look passed between them. 'We can give you a week.'

Prince nodded. 'I'll get back to you.'

With that, he shut the door firmly, then turned to face those around him. Rachel's eyes were wide, Storm's angry. Tori felt her heart pounding in her chest.

'You … you wouldn't, would you?'

Prince smiled at her as he came into the kitchen and lifted Seton from his bouncer. 'Of course not. I'm not going to work for a drug dealer. I'm just keeping my foot in so I can get my hands on one of those mints as evidence.'

Rachel lifted Blythe and carried her into the lounge room to put her on her stomach on the floor.

'So what are we going to do now?' Storm asked the question, but all eyes turned to Tori. She knew they were waiting on her. Waiting for her to trust God and go to the police.

God, help me. I just can't do it. Please give me the courage.

Storm seemed to sense her struggle and took pity on her. 'I know what I'm going to do. That front garden needs weeding. Want to help?'

Gratefully, she nodded. Anything to distract her from her

troubled thoughts. If Storm had planned to distract her, he did a good job of it. He came outside with a singlet top on. She was relieved to see the gash in his shoulder was healing well and tried not to watch as his sun-browned arms pulled weed after weed and dug deep into the soil with a spade.

They worked in companionable silence until Storm moved to the mail box and began pulling out the long grass around the base. Then she heard a giggle. Two teenage girls were walking along the front path with headphones on and both had their eyes fixed on Storm. He gave them a friendly wave and they stopped and came back. Both took off their headphones.

'You're looking hot,' one said, while the other batted her eyelashes.

Storm wiped the sweat from his brow. 'It is fairly warm. You keeping fit, or on your way somewhere?'

The taller one moved closer. 'Thought I might collect some priority mail I've been expecting.'

Storm's mouth turned up in a half smile Tori was sure the girls would find appealing. 'Okay. Hope it's arrived.'

'Oh, it has! I've decided to make it priority anyway.'

The other girl let out a laugh. 'Mail. *Male*. Get it?'

Tori waited for Storm to grunt in disgust, but he just smiled and gave them a wave. 'Have a nice day.' Then he turned and headed her way. She fixed her eyes on the garden, pulling out the weeds with more force than was necessary.

He knelt beside her. She couldn't bring herself to look at him, though she knew he was studying her.

'What's the problem?'

She frowned. 'Why should there be a problem?'

He chuckled and nudged her shoulder with his own. 'You're pulling out those weeds like you want to kill them.'

'They're supposed to die. That's why we're pulling them out.'

So she hadn't hidden her feelings as well as she thought she had.

She made an effort to blank her expression before turning to face him. His eyes were knowing as he looked at her, eyebrows raised.

'What?'

'You tell *me* what.'

She shrugged. 'You just let those girls carry on like idiots and flirt like crazy. It was sickening.'

His brows rose. 'You didn't like them getting my attention?'

'Not like that. They were ridiculous, giggling and carrying on.'

Storm studied her, looking thoughtful. 'At least they showed an interested in me. I might not like how they did it, but they showed they like me.'

Her hands flew to her hips as she flung down the weeds. 'Like you? No, they showed they were infatuated with you.'

'Which makes me feel good. I need some sign, some kind of emotion to respond to. I need to know they feel something.' His dark eyes challenged her.

'They were making fools of themselves, and a fool of you too.'

To her surprise he reached forward and took her chin in his hand. She shook it off and he let it fall to his side, his eyes still holding hers. 'Tori, I used to be just like you. Thought I was better because I didn't let myself feel anything. Thought I was tough; untouchable. It takes a whole lot more courage to show love and emotion knowing you might not be loved in return. It means being open and taking the chance of being hurt. Don't look down on me for being real and trusting.'

She drew in a deep breath as though he had struck her. 'You think I'm a coward?'

'I think you've shut down your emotions. You won't let yourself love or be loved.'

He was right, but she couldn't be vulnerable yet. It was too dangerous.

'Tori, I realised something about Jesus. He loved us, even gave his life for us, knowing that some people,' he looked down, 'like me, would mock him and reject him.' He lifted his eyes to hers again. 'Now I know, that because of that, he was the strongest, bravest man who ever lived!'

His challenge cut her to the heart. If only she could be like Jesus. If only she could be the expressive, openly loving person Storm wanted her to be. No, make that the person *Jesus* wanted her to be.

I just don't think I can do it, Jesus. You're going to have to make a miracle happen in my heart.

***

The next day was one of the most exciting but frightening days of Tori's life. The whole Clements family, including Prince's father, his brothers and sisters, arrived. Along with them was Paul, Rachel's five year old brother, who would soon be coming to live with the family permanently.

Tori's greatest fear was that someone would recognise her. She no longer looked like a boy and there was no hiding the features that had been displayed on front pages of newspapers and news reports around the country.

She stared at the crowd of people in the lounge room, overwhelmed. If only she could busy herself looking after the twins like she did whenever Storm was making her uncomfortable, but the twins had no end of attention and laps to sit in. The chatter was light-hearted and constant and Tori found herself looking from one person to the next, as conversations went on around her.

Blaze, the minister, was the eldest, and he was there with his little girl, Sky. Tori marvelled at how much the girl was an older version of baby Blythe. She could see more similarities in Prince and Sky than she could in Blaze and the little girl.

Storm came to her side. 'Sky is actually Prince's little girl. He had her when he was only sixteen. Her mother abandoned her.'

So Sky was Prince's daughter. She remembered then that Rachel had told her the story. They were planning to take her into the family

171

along with Rachel's little brother once the twins were older.

Watching Sky with Blaze and Bonnie made her wonder how Bonnie would take it. She obviously loved the little girl with her whole heart. She was laughing at something Sky said, and Tori noticed she had amazing blue eyes and a face that glowed.

Despite the beauty, however, her arms and legs displayed scars that left her skin wrinkled, and in Tori's thinking, unsightly. She had been brought up to value physical beauty; her mother taught her it was to be used to demand respect and envy. For the first time in her life she understood how shallow that truly was, and she felt free from the burden of being beautiful. She longed for the glow of happiness Bonnie had, and for a beauty of heart and soul. She wished she could smile again.

Chatter around the table was incessant and Tori looked around, loving the feeling of belonging. Suddenly, she caught the conversation between Storm and one of his sisters. She was the dimpled one with the scar down her cheek. She could have been a model were it not for that scar.

'Misty, tell me about how you got the scar.' Storm's words were surprisingly gentle and subdued. Tori knew him to be the type of person who would come out and say what he was thinking without thought of his tone or how it came across.

The table fell silent. Suddenly everyone seemed to be focused on Misty.

'I fell. It was after a performance and I fell asleep .'

'It was my fault.' The oldest brother, Blaze, leaned forward. 'I was supposed to be watching her.'

Misty shook her head. 'It wasn't your fault. No one knew I had epilepsy then. It was just an accident.'

Storm frowned. 'So I had nothing to do with it?'

The whole family turned to stare at him. 'You?' Misty raised her eyebrows. 'What would you have to do with it? You were only two. I can't even remember if you were there.'

'I think he was.' That was the sister named Beauty.

'What would you remember? You were only two as well.'

'I've got a good memory, though.'

'No, they were already asleep in the van. Dad was with them and Blaze was watching the rest of us.'

The discussion went back and forward amongst the siblings, but Tori was watching Storm's face. A mixture of emotions played across his strong features until he stepped in. 'Do you know Marcos always told me I did it?'

They all turned to stare at him again.

He was now looking at Misty. 'He said I was angry and pushed you then laughed. I've felt so guilty all these years.'

'Oh, Storm.' Misty had tears in her eyes. 'How could he? That horrible man.'

Storm grinned a tentative grin. 'Well, now I know it wasn't me I'll do what I should have done all those years ago.' He stood and came to his sister, taking her into warm embrace. 'I'm sorry, Misty, even though I didn't do it. I'm sorry I shut you out, trying to ignore the guilt of what I didn't even do.'

His family around the table had been stunned into silence. He chuckled. 'I've changed, alright? Don't look at me like I've lost it.'

Still no one spoke and he stepped back and held up his hands as though warding them off. 'I don't want any hugs or drama, but I gave my life to God, alright?'

His request was ignored as the family came for him, crying and laughing all at once as they hugged and swiped at tears. They seemed so comfortable with their emotions; even Storm. But she wanted to run.

'Okay, enough of that.' Misty sniffed and wiped her hand across her nose. 'Let's have some funny in-law stories. The best one gets out of washing up.'

'Be careful, Misty.' Her husband, Roy, had a warning tone to his voice but he was smiling. 'No insults, okay?'

Misty merely grinned. 'You get to talk about Dad, remember? I'm not going to be one sided about this!'

'But he's here. No one's going to talk about someone who's here.'

'And why not?'

It looked as if an argument was about to start, but Storm jumped in first. 'I'll go! I'll go!'

Blaze shook his head at him. 'You're not married, you mug!'

Storm pretended to sulk. 'That's not fair. I need a chance to skip washing up too.'

'As if you were planning on doing it anyway! You don't even pick up your own socks. Rachel does and you think they magically march themselves off to the clothes basket.' Tori spoke without thought and all heads turned to her as the group began to laugh.

'She knows you too well, Storm!' Blaze laughed at his brother. 'You've been found out!'

Storm turned to Tori, ready to retaliate, but she escaped from the room. She shouldn't have let down her guard and allowed herself to become involved. She wasn't a part of this family, no matter how much she wanted to be. She was a child abused by her mother who had no idea about inner beauty or happiness.

In a rare display of anger at her helplessness, she kicked her foot against the kitchen wall. She gasped in pain as a flow of blood began and she rushed to the bathroom to the medicine cupboard. She had to stop the bleeding, then clean up the tell-tale signs on the floor.

***

Storm quietly left the group to find Tori. Her outburst had both surprised and encouraged him. There had been many times he wished Tori would tease him back when he had a go at her, or when he wished she would at least smile or show some kind of response that wasn't calculated and controlled. Now it had finally happened.

'Tori?' He came into the kitchen, then he saw the blood. His heart pounded as he began searching the rooms in the house. *Please God, no.* He heard a sound coming from the bathroom and raced to the closed door. He could hear her scrabbling about in the medicine cupboard. Surely she wasn't back to taking her own life?

He rapped on the door. 'You okay?'

She opened the door to let him in. 'I cut my toe.' She looked embarrassed. 'I tried a band aid but it didn't work.'

Storm nodded, relief overwhelming him as he looked down at the flow of blood coming out through the band aid. 'I can see that.'

'What should I use to clean it up?'

He glanced at the blood trail on the floor. 'Don't worry about it. Let's get you to the hospital.'

She stared at him. 'It's just a cut toe.' She headed back toward the kitchen, but Storm caught her arm.

'Tori, it's not going to stop bleeding by itself. It needs stitches.'

Tori raised her chin. 'I've stopped bleeding without a doctor before, Storm. And do you have any idea what the emergency ward at the hospital is like? I'd be there for hours!'

Storm studied her, undecided, when Prince appeared.

'What's going on?'

Soon the whole family was gathered around Tori, concern etched on their faces.

'What happened?' Misty wanted to know, giving Tori a hug. Storm smiled. Misty wasn't to know that Tori didn't allow most people close enough to show any kind of affection. Trust good old Misty to give her the hug she needed. But his smile faded as he noticed how pale she had become. Was she in shock, or was she simply afraid of going to a public hospital where her identity might be discovered?

The family were all gathered around, talking at once and giving her little choice.

'It definitely needs stitches,' Blaze was saying as he studied it. He stood 'I can take you in, if you like.'

Storm stepped in. 'I will.'

Tori's eyes flew to his and he winked. He knew his tone had an air of determination and authority no one questioned, but still, the family gave Tori encouraging hugs as she exited the house, limping to Storm's car.

Tori was quiet as they travelled in the car, but he knew she was studying him. Finally, she spoke. 'Was that a wink you gave me back there in front of your family?'

He quirked an eyebrow but kept his eye on the road. 'That depends.'

'On what?'

'Did you want it to be?'

He glanced over to see her eyes widen and a faint trace of red work its way into her cheeks. He'd made her blush! He was beginning to think she was human after all. He liked her human side.

'Watch out, Tori,' he said quietly. 'You're starting to go all soft on me.'

She glared at him. 'Like you haven't done that yourself. I saw the way your family looked at you in shock when you showed a bit of emotion.'

He grinned. 'You're doing well.'

She folded her arms across her chest and he grinned wider. At least he'd distracted her from her fear.

Chapter Twenty-Three

The emergency waiting room was busy, just as Tori had predicted. Storm glanced around at all the people, then back to Tori's toe, covered in a tea towel. They moved their way toward the triage nurse.

'Next.'

Tori kept her eyes down so Storm gave his own name to the nurse. He tried to prepare himself for any questions that might come up, but thankfully, none did. He gave his own card and details and chuckled at the irony of it. He'd been so angry when he'd realised Tori had been using his name and pretending to be him. Now here he was, doing it for her.

They moved to the waiting room and sat down. He turned to her, but she had withdrawn into herself again. The openness of the past hour was gone. Frustration rose up within him. He'd watched the way his family hugged her and had a burning desire to do the same. But she was so comfortable with pain, so comfortable with fighting, and so self-sufficient. It was affection that made her vulnerable and love that threw her into emotional turmoil. Storm suspected she would prefer he hit her than draw her into an embrace.

Could he ever change her? He doubted it. If she had any idea of the affection he was beginning to feel for her, she would run the other way.

'You angry with me?' he asked, his tone gruff as though he didn't really care.

She stared at him, not answering for a moment.

He grinned. 'Go on, say it.'

'Say what?' Her expression was carefully blank.

'Say, yes, you forced me to come here to the hospital—a public, dangerous place where questions could be asked and I could be discovered.' His voice lowered. 'Or else say, no, all I feel is a strange kind of stirring in my heart. I've found a family who cares for me. I don't know why, but they treat me like I'm special and yes, maybe they even love me.'

She looked away and he wished he could shake her. No, he didn't. He wished he could hug her. He didn't want anyone to lay violent hands on her ever again.

He looked sideways at her and chuckled. 'You'll forgive me when you become a foot model.'

'Foot model?' Her green eyes flew to his.

'Yeah, you know, they'll hire you to be in movies or ads where they need nice feet.'

***

Tori tried to screw up her nose at him, but failed as a smile began to form. 'You're an idiot sometimes.'

'It gets me by.' He nudged her shoulder with a grin.

A man wearing blue strode out from behind the double doors. 'Storm Clements.'

Storm quirked an eyebrow at her. 'Shall I go or shall you?' He grabbed her hand. 'I know; let's both go.'

She bit her lip, feeling a strange pulling sensation at the sides of her mouth. Muscles she hadn't used for a long time were moving and stretched to their full width. Storm hadn't seen it, as he was focused on the doctor, but she knew a miracle had just happened. She had smiled.

Storm's arm slid around her waist and the smile disappeared as she looked up at him. What was he doing? Of course, he was helping her walk. She leaned against him. He felt strong and capable and she felt secure.

'Up here.' The doctor pointed to a bed. Before she could move forward, Storm had put his arm under her knees and lifted her onto the bed, carefully lowering her down. If her silly heart would stop its pounding she would know what to do, how to respond, but she couldn't think. She didn't even flinch as the needle went in.

***

Storm watched Tori in fascination. She'd built up such a resistance to pain he didn't doubt her ability to cope with any injury she ever came up against. It bothered him that she had a need to do that, but what bothered him more was her resistance to love. Emotionally, she didn't allow herself to be hurt, but neither did she allow herself to be loved or appreciated. She was missing out on life.

The knowledge left him with an ache that kept him awake late into that night. He sat alone in Prince and Rachel's empty lounge room, quiet now all the family had left, and prayed.

The door opened and there she was. Her clear green eyes settled on him before she limped into the room.

He patted the lounge beside him but she headed to the opposite side.

'I can't sleep.'

'In pain?'

She looked confused, then recognition lit her eyes as she glanced to her toe. 'No. Just … thinking.'

'About?'

'Your family. I like them.' She took a deep breath. 'And about going to the police. I'm hoping Prince finds some kind of evidence to use so he doesn't need me.'

'Me too.'

She lowered herself into the lounge opposite him and he looked at her a moment before picking up the deck of cards on

179

the table. 'A game?'

She tucked her legs up under her and studied his fingers as he shuffled the deck of cards.

'Do you know "Up and down the river"?'

When she shook her head, he came and sat beside her. He ignored the way she stared at him. 'Let me show you.'

He moved closer. She sat perfectly still, not moving a muscle, but watching intently as he dealt her hand, face up. He knew she was aware of the way his arm rested against hers. He began to explain, his face close, his eyes looking directly into hers. He could see she wasn't listening and fear was flickering through her eyes.

'What are you doing, Storm?' she finally asked, her voice coming out hoarse.

'Teaching you cards.'

Her eyes challenged him and he smiled into them.

'Please don't,' she whispered when his hand came up to tuck a stray wisp of hair behind her ear.

'Why?'

The question was without reprimand and gentle. She didn't answer and his eyes didn't waver from hers. 'I need a good answer, Tori, because I'm finding it hard to keep my distance without one.'

When she didn't answer, he took a risk. He put down the card in his hand, then reached for her, drawing her against his chest in a comforting, unthreatening way. Yet he knew she felt threatened. Her heart pounded and she trembled. What would it take to heal her? To allow her to live life to the full? Life was not fully lived without experiencing all the senses and that included feelings.

It was then it hit him. He was living life to the full. The feelings he had for Tori Seeth were strong and they were ... love. Soppy, annoying affection, but something so much deeper too.

A year ago he would have been disgusted with himself. Now he just smiled. *Thanks God, for love. Show me what to do with it.*

***

Tori needed to escape. There was no space to think or protect herself. And yet at the same time, there was something about Storm's closeness that she longed for. Confusion washed through her and her heart beat hard and fast, but she didn't want to move.

'I wish I could take your pain, Tori,' he said softly, down into her hair, 'but Prince says only God can heal like that.'

'I'm okay.'

She felt rather than saw him shake his head. 'You're not. It's almost superhuman the way you can shut out any emotion or feeling. I thought you were tough at first, but now …'

She pulled quickly back from him, staring him down. 'But now?'

'I can see you're holding onto it out of fear and it makes you miss out on feeling loved or valuable. You've shut out the world.'

Tori couldn't deny it, but for a moment she wished she knew how to love and be loved in return. She felt something for Storm Clements she'd never felt before in her life and she was afraid of losing him.

She forced herself to move toward him and put her arms around his neck. But as her mouth came toward his, he broke away. Tori stared at him, relieved and afraid all at once.

'That's not what I was asking from you, Tori.' His sun-browned hand came up to touch her cheek and take the sting from his rejection.

She longed to ask him what he was asking for, but the words wouldn't come. And in her heart, she knew. He was asking for the kind of love his family had. A love she couldn't offer him because she'd never known it before in her life.

It's God's love, she thought as she watched Storm pack up the cards and put them away. *The love that made Jesus die for me when I didn't even know he existed.*

181

His dark eyes rested on her as he stood. 'I think we should try to get some sleep.'

She nodded, but she sat alone on the lounge for a long time after he had gone to bed.

Chapter Twenty-Four

'Tori, you've got to see this!'

Tori managed to sit up in bed, rubbing her eyes. Storm was at the foot of her bed, holding his phone.

'What is it?'

He came and sat beside her on the bed. 'It's your father.'

'What?'

'Look.' He came closer and pressed the triangular play icon in the middle of his phone screen. 'Listen.'

A news reporter moved onto the screen. 'And today I have with me, Russel Farlow, the father of Victoria Seeth, the teenager who mysteriously disappeared after allegedly murdering a girl and then turning on her own mother.'

Tori's ears began to buzz as a man appeared on the screen. He was a stranger, and yet something about him was familiar. Somewhere in the haze of her mind she was aware of Storm's hand reaching for hers.

'I am asking anyone who has any idea where my daughter is, to please come forward. And Victoria, if you are out there, please turn yourself in. I don't care what you've done. I'm your father and I've only just heard of your existence. Your mother kept it from me all these years and I hate the thought of never meeting you. I wish I could have been there for you. Whatever you've been through, you are my daughter, my own flesh and blood, and from now on I will be here for you.' His voice caught. 'I promise.'

Tori's heart pounded. She felt as though time had stopped still. Why had she believed her mother? Of course she had lied. She always lied. Her father hadn't even known she existed!

Storm left her to herself and she sat for a long time, overwhelmed. Could she trust her father? What if her mother was believed? Would her father still support her? Was it worth the risk of turning herself in? Finally she threw off her blankets and got up, but she was in a daze. She went through the motions of getting dressed then wandered out into the lounge room. Seton and Blythe were lying on the floor and they smiled up at her as she arrived. A soft voice came from the next room and she stopped. The voice was mesmerising and was soon joined by the piano. That piano hadn't been touched since she arrived, but she knew it was Rachel playing. She strained to listen to the words.

'Clinging to the rainbow,
I know your promise stands,
your sky is lit by sunset
held in loving hands.

At times it disappears yet
I know my eyes can't see
all life's eternal moments
you have planned for me.

Clinging to your promise
I know you rose on high
and in the morning I will
behold the dawn lit sky.

Yes, clinging to the rainbow
although it may be night,
I know your promise stands

in everlasting light.'

Clinging to the promise,
Your love has given me,
That I will live forever,
I'm yours eternally.

Tori swallowed back a lump in her throat. The beauty of the words and voice had touched her somewhere deep inside. Even if she was jailed, God knew the truth and nothing could take away God's love for her. Nothing could take away the promise of her eternal home with him – the first one who had ever truly loved her.

A baby moved at her feet and she looked down. Blythe had managed to roll over far enough that her head was now under the lounge. Tori reached to gently pull her out. The little girl was sucking her fist. Or was it just her fist? No, there was something white and crinkly and plastic. She must have found it hiding under the lounge. It was probably rubbish that had been sitting there for a long time. It would be hard for a vacuum cleaner to reach, but a baby's arm could slip under there easily.

'Give me that, little girl.' Tori worked Blythe's fingers open, then stared in horror. It was a mint! A Happy Kingdom Church mint. It was still in its wrapper, but what if it hadn't been? What if the baby had swallowed the mint and ingested a drug? What if it had killed her?

A cry formed somewhere down inside. How many babies and vulnerable people were still in danger because she had been too selfish, too scared of losing her own freedom, to expose the truth? She turned the plastic packet over in her hand. Then finally, she broke down and cried. She cried for the loss of love, emotion and security, and most of all for her inability to trust God. She'd known she should give herself up to authorities, but she hadn't been able to trust God with her life. Now she knew she couldn't trust herself with her life. She'd let drug dealers continue to destroy lives and get rich.

'God, forgive me!'

'Tori?'

It was Rachel, followed by Prince and Storm. She realised they had heard her cries. For the first time in her life, she initiated a hug as she ran and clung to Rachel with all she had. Then, with shaking hands she held out the mint.

'Blythe was sucking on it. It was under the lounge.'

Prince's face paled as he bent to lift Blythe from the floor and hold her protectively to his chest. 'I must have dropped it there.'

Rachel looked devastated. 'Or it could have come from the nappy bag. I put one in there ages ago. I need to vacuum better. It never even crossed my mind that she would reach under the lounge.'

Storm shook his head at all of them. 'Guys, stop the "what ifs". God gave you your mint, didn't he? You have evidence.'

Tori nodded wiping at red eyes. 'He did. And I'm ready to go to the police. I'm going to trust him, whatever happens like I should have a long time ago.'

Storm stepped forward and looked deep into her eyes. 'You sure?'

'Yes.'

'Do you want me to take you?'

She nodded, drawing strength from his arm now around her shoulder. He knew a large part of her story. He'd been with her through it and she wanted and needed him right now. If she was locked up it might be the last time she saw him for a long time.

She trembled as she related her story to the police, but at the same time, she felt excitement and peace.

The police officer closed the file with a nod. 'Your mother has already been arrested and charged with murder, but your statement certainly helps.'

Tori's eyes widened. 'But … when?'

'Only this morning. A boy named Patrick came forward with evidence, along with Sarah's father.'

Mick. Of course. Mick knew what her mother was like. He had experienced her violence.

'We need you to stay in the area until things are sorted out with the Happy Kingdom Church. But your father is desperate to meet you. Are you okay with that?'

She had a father who wanted her! The knowledge was still too much to comprehend.

Storm's hand squeezed hers and she realised with a start that she hadn't answered. She managed to pull herself together. 'Yes! Yes, I'd like to meet him please.'

The police officer smiled at her enthusiasm. 'Where would you like to meet up? He has to fly from interstate but believes he can get here later today.'

Storm stepped forward. 'They can meet at my brother's place where we've been staying.' He gave the address and phone number then turned to Tori with a smile. 'Looks like you're going to meet your dad today.'

Her dad. Hope and joy spilled out of her heart and through her veins. Dazed, she just looked at Storm, unable to speak.

'You're free to go now.' The officer looked amused when she took a moment to draw her eyes away from Storm to pay attention. 'But I don't think you're in the best frame of mind to be on the road right now. If you drove here, I'd recommend you let your boyfriend drive you home.'

Boyfriend? His words jarred her back to reality. She saw the way Storm's brows flew to his hairline before he glanced down to his hand holding hers, but he didn't say anything. When he caught her eye, boldness welled up within her and she winked. His mouth dropped open in shock and she felt triumphant. She never thought anything would shock the ever-calm and in control Storm Clements.

***

The doorbell pealed and Prince looked up. It was too early for it to be Tori's father. Tori was already pacing the lounge room floor, but they weren't expecting him for a few hours yet. Rachel was playing the piano and singing, just softly because the twins were asleep. He loved the sound.

He opened the door and stopped still. Deborah and Parker stood there. He didn't like the look in their eyes. His heart began to pound.

'We'd like you to come to the church office to discuss some things.'

His mind raced. Was it safe to insist they discussed it here? With Rachel and the twins here? With Storm and Tori?

He eyed them carefully. 'What kind of things?'

'We've had the police asking a few questions. We think it would be in your best interest to prepare your responses so that you aren't implicated in anything you'd prefer not to be.'

It was a threat. 'I'll just let Rach know where I'm going.'

'No you won't. You're not involving her this time. Leave her a note and say you've just popped out for a few minutes.'

He was handed a slip of paper and a pen. His eyes slid shut. *God, I need your help here.*

His hand writing was as steady as he could make it. *I've just slipped out for half an hour. Back soon, Prince.* He wrote the words they directed him to, and sat it on the hall table. Then he quietly followed them out the door.

He tried to pray. He was too overwhelmed and only three words would come. *Help me, God.*

His thoughts went to Rachel and the twins. He loved them so much! But whatever happened, God would carry them through. God was trustworthy.

He was led into the church office where Parker pulled out a chair and pushed him into it. He looked at the two controlling

188

people standing over him. But they weren't in control. God was.

Suddenly he could pray. Words flowed from his heart and mouth and he only realised he was praying aloud, in another language, when Deborah stepped backward. Her eyes flew to the wrapped mint sitting on the desk beside him.

'Did you have one?' She interrupted his prayer.

'No.'

'Then why? Why are you doing this?'

'What? Praying?'

'Yes, faking the tongues.'

Faking them? Is that what they all did? He guessed the psychotic drugs made it easier. He hadn't had a mint. So did that mean what he thought it meant? He had the gift of tongues, the real gift of tongues given by God, and he hadn't even known it. When he had been too overwhelmed to pray, God's Holy Spirit had prayed for him. He began to smile as peace which transcended all understanding filled his heart and mind.

Deborah seemed shaken, but Parker stepped forward and his eyes, once so warm, were cold and hard.

'We know someone in your family went to the police. So here's how it goes. We tell them you knew about the mints all along and agreed to be a part of our business. Otherwise, how are you going to explain why you received so much pay for so little work these last few months? The extra was obviously for your drug dealing, but your wife didn't know. Even Kenny will testify that you handed him those blankets on occasion.'

So they had covered themselves all along. There was a reason for his ridiculously high pay. It wasn't God's blessings for those who followed him. It was the manipulation of a group calling themselves the Happy Kingdom Church.

Parker was now leaning forward, his breath on his face, his eyes glaring into his. 'Or the other option is—'

He was cut off by a pounding on the door. He stiffened, a

look of terror passing through his eyes as a young man wearing a hooded jacket burst in waving a gun toward his face.

'Sent the police after me, did you?' The man stood, legs apart, both hands now holding the gun, finger on the trigger.

Deborah paled. 'Kenny. Of course not.'

'You did too! You framed me all along so that I'd get the rap if you got caught. You and your promises of money and mansions.'

Prince swallowed hard. Kenny didn't look rational. Parker seemed to realise it too. His pupils were dilated, his breathing ragged.

'Kenny, they aren't empty promises.'

Kenny laughed a high pitched, crazed laugh as he took a step closer to Parker. 'You still think you can fool me?'

'Kenny.' Parkers voice held a warning. 'Settle down.'

Kenny snorted. 'Or what? You'll call the police? Hey, I've got a great idea. Why don't we call them? Try fooling them with your grand stories why don't you?'

His eyes darted from Parker and Deborah then rested on Prince. Still holding the gun in one hand he took a phone from his pocket and threw it to Prince. 'Call them. Now. Or you'll get a bullet in your head.'

Prince didn't hesitate. He bent his head and concentrated on the phone. He could hear Parker's voice in the background. 'Prince, don't do it. I'm warning you.'

Desperately he tried to steady his fingers and work out how to use Kenny's phone. As he pressed the emergency number, the phone was thrown from his hand. He gasped. Parker had leapt forward and landed hard against him. He was now lying on the floor, grasping for the phone, but Kenny was there first.

'Hello? Police? I'm at the Happy Kingdom Church office. I've got a drug lord bailed up here, shaking in his boots 'cause I'm dobbing him in. Can you get down here real quick? Don't know how long I can hold the crazy man.'

As he spoke, Deborah edged back toward the desk behind

them. Prince felt his heart beat faster. She was up to something. Her hand reached toward a drawer, but Kenny spun around, dropping his phone.

'No, don't move, crazy drug lady.' He waved the gun at her, then pointed it to where Parker was now sitting on the floor beside Prince. 'Go on, join him.'

Deborah ignored him and flung the drawer open. At the same time an explosion came from the gun and hit the desk. She threw her arm back, shocked.

'I told you.' Kenny's eyes were narrowed. 'I know how to shoot a gun.' He moved to the desk and looked in the drawer. He pulled out another gun. 'Interesting.' He now pointed one at Parker and one at Deborah. 'Move together, both of you. You were in this together, you'll end it together.' He laughed as though he'd told a wonderful joke.

Prince hoped the police would arrive before the young man totally lost it. His hands were becoming more unsteady by the minute and his eyes now appeared dull. He recognised the effect of the Happy Kingdom mints. He'd been through it often enough himself, albeit unknowingly.

Kenny trained his gun on them, but his eyes kept darting to the door. Then, setting one of the guns down he fumbled in his pocket and pulled out a mint. He passed it to Prince. 'Here, unwrap this for me, would ya?'

Prince shook his head. 'Do you really want it? They're not worth it, Kenny. They give you a high for a while, but it feels pretty awful when you come down.'

Kenny nodded. 'You're right. Hey, give it to one of them. They're going to feel rotten soon. Give them a last chance of happiness before they go down.'

Prince did as he was told, but Parker threw it to the ground and spat in his face. The hate oozing from the man shook him. Why hadn't he seen it before?

Kenny moved closer and studied Prince. 'He hates you too? Are you trying to get out too? What lies did he tell you?'

Prince shook his head. 'Too many. But I didn't know I was dealing drugs. I'm so sorry I gave them to you, Kenny.'

Kenny looked taken aback. 'Why should you care?'

A deep, heartfelt sigh came from inside Prince before he could stop it. 'Because Jesus' love is real and this church have used his name and abused your trust.'

Kenny paused, his eyes turning thoughtful. Then he shrugged. 'Don't worry about it, mate. I knew what I was getting into. It was my own stupid choice. Thought I could get myself a better life. I never believed any of their Jesus stuff, anyway. I just pretended because I had to, to get the drugs.'

Prince looked at him earnestly. 'But Kenny, what if that was the only true thing they ever said, even if they themselves don't believe it?'

Kenny tilted his head to the side. 'Now you've got me thinking, man.' He laughed, though his manner was more rational, now. 'I guess I'll have plenty of time to think on it sitting in that prison cell.'

Parker leaned forward, but stopped when Kenny waved the gun at him again. Still, he spoke. 'Listen to me, Kenny. You let us go now and we can all escape.'

'Escape to what?' Kenny looked amused. 'A life back on the streets? Prison will be like a mansion to me anyway, after living on the streets. Three meals a day, a clean, dry place to sleep.' He grinned. 'I'm off to my mansion, mate. Don't try to take it away from me with any more of your stupid lies.' He stood as sirens came down the street. 'Oh look, here's my royal carriage now.'

Prince held his breath, wondering what Parker and Deborah would do. They were unusually subdued. They didn't even speak when the officers came in and handcuffed them. Kenny calmly handed his gun to the officers and pointed to Prince.

'He's not part of it. He's the only decent human being in this room.'

The officer nodded. 'Just the same, we'll need to take him in for questioning.'

Kenny tilted his head. 'Yeah, I guess so. Since he's the only one you'll get any truth out of.'

Prince tried to hide his amusement. Kenny was quite a character and today he may just have saved his life. His thoughts flew to Rachel. She must be worried.

'Can I phone my wife? She doesn't know where I am.'

The officer smiled. 'Actually, she does. We got a hysterical phone call from her saying she thought you'd been taken against your will. But I'll just give her a call and let her know you're safe, then we'll head to the station.'

Once he had been interviewed and signed his statement, Prince was driven home by the police.

He was hugged and cried over the moment he stepped in the door. Everyone was talking at once.

Prince laughed as he hugged them all and allowed himself to be hugged. He was so blessed. Not by a greedy, manipulating church, but by God.

***

The drama had settled down and Prince had shared his story. Time seemed to drag by.

Tori was grateful for Storm's company. Her father was due any moment, but she didn't feel she could wait a minute longer.

She paced until Storm's strong hand reached out to encompass hers and pull her down onto the lounge beside him. She tried to sit still but found herself wriggling on the cushion like a small child. Storm shot her the occasional amused grin.

'Settle,' he said, but she knew it was not really a reprimand, but an acknowledgement of her desperation to see her father.

Finally a knock came at the door. Tori froze. Storm gave her hand a squeeze before going to answer. She stared through the open doorway, knowing that any moment her father would stand in front of her. A father who said he wanted her. But why? Would he be anything like her mother? Would he abuse her? Would she be better off just living on her own?

Footsteps sounded along the hall and she stiffened. A man stepped into the room and allowed his eyes to meet Tori's. He had the most understanding eyes she'd ever seen.

He took a deep breath, then smiled. 'Victoria? I'm your father.' His voice was deep and kind.

'Dad.' Her voice came out in a whisper and she felt her eyes filling with tears. 'Please call me Tori.'

'Tori.' He said the name softly, tenderly. Then he came closer. 'I'm so sorry. I had no idea what you were going through. I didn't even know I had you. It wasn't until your mother came on the news and details were given that I realised you had to be mine. And when I saw the picture of you, well, then I knew.'

She gazed up into his understanding eyes. Green eyes just like hers and a heart-shaped face so like hers. It was obvious they were related.

'I believe you that you didn't know. Mum is very good at deceit.' She hoped her words reassured him. Both of them had suffered because of her mother's lies.

They just looked at one another for a few moments before Tori sat down, her father following suit. He was nothing like she'd imagined from her mother's angry, bitter words. She'd expected someone as rough and heartless as she. Instead, he looked like the kind of father any girl would want; the type of man you could trust to try to do what was best for you. She suspected by his clothes that he also made a decent living for himself. 'Do you have a family?'

He nodded. 'Yes. I'm married. Melissa is my wife, and I have three children … four, including you.'

Tori was about to ask their names when she realised something. 'Mum never even told me your name. I heard it for the first time this morning on that news report.'

He smiled and seemed to relax as he held out a hand for her to shake. 'I'm Russell William Farlow and I'm your father.'

Tori smiled as she spoke in the same formal tone her father had. 'And I am Victoria Anne Seeth, your daughter. But I'd like to go by the name Tori Farlow, if that's okay.'

He nodded, smiling. 'It would be an honour for you to take my name. So now we have the formalities out of the way, let's talk!'

Tori could have listened to her father all day. She learned he was a successful businessman who had been her mother's boyfriend in their university days. Their relationship had deteriorated quickly once Russell discovered her violent temper and drinking problem. He later married Melissa, and now had Ben, twelve, Rebecca ten, and Laura, five.

'Ben is a gifted sportsman.' Her father spoke with obvious pride. 'He's the fastest twelve year old in his school. And Rebecca is our artistic one. She loves to draw and paint, and some of her artwork is brilliant. As for Laura, all she wants to do is model or act. She's a natural and she has the perfect little face for it.'

Tori's heart plummeted. 'You know, it's not all it's cut out to be, don't you? The modelling and acting business.'

Her father looked at her with interest, then listened, spellbound, as she told her story, describing her many experiences, the jealousies, the hard work, the superficial beauty she so often saw idolised when the value of the heart and soul was ignored.

'I don't think I would want anyone I know or love to get involved in it.' She grasped his hand. 'I don't want Laura to be taken in by the whole modelling culture. It's so shallow and empty.'

He nodded in understanding. 'Then you'd better meet your sister and explain it to her. Laura was so excited to think of having a half-sister. She would be here with me now if I'd let her come.'

She looked at him hopefully. 'I'd love to meet her.'

'I have to get back tonight, but you're welcome to come and stay with us as soon as you're ready.'

'Your wife wouldn't mind?'

He smiled. 'No. She told me to make sure I invited you.'

Excitement filled her and she felt something she'd never felt before as the man in front of her reached over and gave her a fatherly hug. She had found her family. She had found somewhere she belonged.

She would tell them about God as soon as she could. After being denied the truth for so many years she would now speak the truth with love and conviction to anyone who would listen. A gentle knock came on the lounge room door and Tori looked up to see Storm standing there. She gasped.

'I can't believe I forgot about you.'

'Me either.' He pretended to look disgusted but failed miserably.

She shook her head. She'd tied up Prince and Rachel's lounge room for over an hour without a thought.

Storm looked at her father. 'You said your flight leaves at five? Prince said he can drive you back to the airport.'

He nodded his thanks and Storm backed out of the room. 'I'll leave you two to your goodbyes.'

Her father smiled. 'I'm surprised you wanted to spend so much time with your old man when you have someone like him out there waiting for you. The police filled me in on some of the details. It seems he saved your life.'

Tori smiled. 'He is pretty special.'

She gave him a fierce hug and he clung back with equal strength.

'I love you, Tori.'

She heard his whispered words, but couldn't respond for the lump in her throat.

Prince poked his head in the door, jingling the keys in his hand. 'We ready to go?'

Tori nodded and forced out the words she so badly wanted to say. 'Goodbye, Dad. Love you. See you soon.'

She waved him off at the door, then wandered back into the lounge room.

Storm stood there and he smiled as she approached. His eyes showed he was amused about something. 'So I'm pretty special, am I?'

She stopped short. She hadn't meant for him to hear.

'It's okay.' His mouth turned up in the corners and his eyes twinkled. 'I am pretty special. I'm surprised it took you so long to work it out.'

'Don't make fun of me.' Warmth filled her cheeks as embarrassment overwhelmed her. 'I never … I don't usually say things like that.'

Storm stopped her words with a hug. 'It's okay. You're pretty special too.'

She looked up at him and smiled. His eyes fixed on her as though he couldn't tear his gaze away. She bit her lip as his whole expression changed. She couldn't define it, except to say that in that moment he looked at her differently; he swallowed hard and his eyes softened. Years of modelling had numbed her to the admiring stares, but Storm's look went deeper, warming her heart. There was a lot to be said for inner beauty and joy; something only God's love could give.

'You smiled. About time.' His voice was gruff and she grinned at him. He was getting worse and worse at trying to hide his feelings. In fact, she would dare to say his cover had been completely blown. But so had hers.

Chapter Twenty-Five

Storm listened as Tori relayed her time with her father.

'He said I can go and live with them. And Storm, they're going to be there to support me through the court cases.'

Her eyes were wide with the wonder of it and Storm smiled. Of course they would be. This animated, expressive Tori was captivating.

'I won't be scared when I'm called to testify against Mum. Dad will be there. And God. Why didn't I trust him earlier?'

Her eyes looked sad for a moment and Storm remembered the girl he'd first met, who looked like a ragged boy with haunted, troubled eyes, a body malnourished and all bones. He was going to miss her.

'I finally belong somewhere, Storm.' She smiled as he looked into her eyes. He had no idea why her mother had insisted on her wearing blue contact lenses when the green was so clear and pretty. His eyes dropped to her smiling mouth. Perfectly symmetrical lips framed even, white teeth. It was amazing what a smile could do. Amazing what love, hope and acceptance could do.

'The police said it's okay for me to go and stay with Dad now Deborah and Parker have been arrested.'

He didn't hear her words at first, but as they registered, it was bittersweet.

She threw her arms around his neck and gave him a fierce hug. 'Thanks so much for all you've done. For saving my life, for sharing your family, for showing me I do have a reason to live. Whatever happens I'll never forget you.'

Storm found he couldn't speak. He wanted to ask her to stay, but that would be selfish. She had her family now and she needed to get to know them. If he could think of a reason to go with her he would, but she didn't need him any longer. He had begun to think she might have feelings for him, but maybe he had read her wrong. If only he had more time to work it out. It was all happening too fast.

As he said goodbye and she caught the taxi to the airport the following day, he thought on how nice it had been to be needed. No, it was more than that. For the first time in his life he cared for someone more than himself. He'd respected and yes, loved Tori as he'd never loved another person in his life. He would go back to work in the circus now, but he doubted he would ever be the same again.

***

Rachel stood beside Prince, watching as Storm took first his niece, then his nephew in his arms. Both giggled and smiled at him, wrapping their pudgy hands around his neck.

Storm kissed them both on the cheek, then handed them back to Prince and Rachel. 'I love you, you little terrors.'

Prince grinned. 'They're going to miss you, Storm.'

He looked pained. 'I'm going to miss them too.' He shook his head. 'What have you people done to me? I've turned all soft!'

Rachel laughed outright. 'A nice soft, though.'

He grunted and shook his head before picking up his bag and climbing into his car.

Rachel forced down the lump in her throat as he drove away. She'd always had a soft spot for the unapproachable Storm Clements.

She turned to Prince. 'I'm going to miss Storm. And Tori, too.' She bit her lip. 'Prince, what do you think about fostering children?'

His eyes widened and he laughed as he pointed to Blythe. The little girl was grabbing at Rachel's ear rings. 'Let's see if we can manage our own two, first.'

She chuckled. 'I don't mean today. I mean sometime in the future. I've just been thinking about what Tom and Carol said that day at church. Maybe our home is meant to be a haven for the lost and broken. Girls like Tori. From what Tori told me, foster homes can be pretty awful. Maybe we can offer a real place of refuge and love for foster children.'

Prince nodded. 'It's certainly worth praying about!'

Rachel agreed. It was. She often pondered Carol's words in her heart. Unlike Deborah's forceful claims, something about Carol's words rang true that day. She doubted she would have felt peace about harbouring Tori if those words hadn't been spoken. But would she have sent Storm and Tori away? She looked up at Prince. 'What do you think will happen between Storm and Tori now?'

Prince smiled. 'I think that now the storm is over the rainbow will come out. I just hope Storm clings to the hope of the rainbow.'

Rachel smiled back, burying her head in his shirt and laughing as Blythe reached from his arms and grabbed her hair. She disentangled her daughter's fingers.

'God's promises are amazing, aren't they?' she whispered. 'His promise of salvation if we will just believe; his promise of forgiveness; his promise to always be here with us. I will never look at a rainbow in the same way again. Even through the storm, God's promises will hold. The rainbow will always come.'

Prince nodded. 'Hey, did you ever think about the fact that without the storm there would be no rainbow?'

'No,' Rachel admitted, 'but just the same, I don't think I'll be hoping for the storms.'

Prince chuckled his agreement.

Chapter Twenty-Six

Storm followed the news closely, always recording it if he had a circus performance at the time it was on. There were continual updates on the 'Victoria Seeth mystery' as it was labelled by the media. The controversial case went through the courts with as much drama as Tori had expected. Her mother was so used to living a lie her stories were convincing, but the evidence piled against her until finally she was put behind bars permanently.

'How do you feel about this victory?' the reporters asked Tori as she left the final hearing.

Tori looked serious. 'There's no victory in seeing my mother's denial and pain. The only victory has been in me finding a new family, a new life, and a new faith in God.'

'So you forgive your mother?' a reporter asked.

Tori's expression became pained for a moment, then she nodded. 'I will work at it every day of my life.'

'And will you go back to modelling?'

At that, Tori didn't hesitate. 'Never. There are so many more worthwhile things I can do with my life.'

***

The court cases were over and Tori was restless. She loved staying with her father and his family, but she knew it was time to earn her own way.

She wanted to find the hairdresser who'd first cut her hair into the Storm Clements style and pay her. That's what Jesus would want her to do. She also wanted to pay the Salvation Army store for all she'd stolen during her time on the run. The Salvation Army was known for the way it cared for the homeless and drug dependant and showed them Jesus. She would love to donate as much to them as she possibly could.

But first, she needed a job. She curled a finger around a strand of hair, now long, shiny and healthy again. Where should she go? Her heart cried out to be wherever Storm was.

She missed him but wasn't game to contact him. Since her emotions had returned to normal, she struggled to control them, and the last thing she wanted was for Storm to know just how deeply she felt for him; she wanted to set him free from her dependence on him so he could know his life was his own. He didn't need to care for a vulnerable, hurting teenager any longer.

If only she could shake him from her mind. She'd prayed for release from her feelings for him, but they wouldn't leave. In fact, they grew stronger.

What am I meant to do, God? Please help me to know.

***

Storm straightened his outfit, knowing he looked impressive. All eyes were on him as he strode into the ring. Dusty Lane stood perfectly still, waiting. With a running leap, he did a flip and landed on the horse's back. Cheers erupted. With practised ease he stood, held out his arms and motioned for Dusty Lane to canter. Years of teamwork came together, reminding him of a flowing river, smooth and beautiful.

It was when his hands met Dusty Lane's broad back and his feet reached up to the sky that he thought he saw her. Just a quick, upside down glimpse. But how could he know for sure? He was mid-handstand on the back of a cantering horse.

God, you have to get her out of my mind.

He faltered. He'd never faltered before. When he stood back on the ground and the audience erupted into applause he scanned the faces. There was no sign of her.

He headed back to his van. Time to change into his normal clothes. He passed the tiger's cage and stopped. Now he *was* going crazy. It looked like she was standing there by the cage near his van where he had first seen her. But she didn't look like she was trying to be Storm Clements. She was wearing a skort with a pretty turquoise top that made her eyes shine the same colour. Those eyes danced but her smile was uncertain.

She spoke his name. He couldn't possibly be hearing things too, could he?

She took a hesitant step toward him and slowly his face split into a grin. 'Tori Seeth! What are you doing here?' He tried to sound gruff. It didn't work.

'Actually, I'm Tori Farlow now.'

He came to stand directly in front of her, drawn by a longing he couldn't ignore. 'Tori Seeth, then Storm Clements, then Tori Farlow. Who do you plan to be next?'

She shrugged, her face turning a pretty shade of pink. This was no daydream. Everything about her was so alive! Her hair had grown. It shone in soft waves around her shoulders. He wanted to touch it. Shoving his hands in his pockets, he tilted his head. 'So you're not trying to be Storm Clements again?'

She smiled. 'No. I have to admit I've missed him, though.'

'I thought you would be too busy with your new life and new family and all.'

Her earnest green eyes became uncertain and her voice shook slightly. 'I told you, I'll never forget you, Storm.'

Unable to resist, he reached out and gave her a hug. To his surprise, she snuggled into his arms, seeming content to stay there. She hadn't answered his first question.

He moved back so he could see her, but rested his hands on her waist, just needing to touch her. 'So why are you here?'

'Can you believe Brindley contacted me? He saw me on the news and offered me a job. I'm going to be doing the circus books. I've always loved maths. He said I can do an online accounting course at the same time.'

'Seriously?'

She nodded and her eyes danced. 'See, he has this new performer and he's getting way more money than he used to. He needs someone to deal with it.' Her voice became breathless. 'I saw you in there. You're unbelievable!'

For a moment he couldn't speak. Her eyes were shining with admiration and … love?

He took a risk, drawing her back into his embrace. 'I realised something in there tonight, Tori. You're the only one I really want to impress.'

'Me?' Her voice was close to a squeak.

He grinned, liking the way her arms tightened around him and her eyes stared up into his. 'Yes, you. So what now?'

'What now?'

'Mm hm. I'm hoping you can tell me.'

'I don't know. First I need to earn some money. I want to pay the people I stole from.'

'Oh?'

'The hairdresser who gave me the Storm Clements haircut, the shop I got my clothes from,' she bit her lip, 'and Trainlink. I forgot about my train rides. I got really good at evading fairs and dodging ticket inspectors.'

She would really do that? He was impressed. 'I can come with you, if you like.'

Her mouth turned up at the corners. 'I'd like that. I should have enough money in two weeks, after my first pay.' She shuffled her feet. 'So are you going to be performing here for a while?'

'Of course. If you're here.' He gave her his best boyish grin. 'I wouldn't want to miss out on the next phase of my exciting life, would I now *Storm*?'

She let out a laugh. It was a spontaneous, joyful sound and Storm knew she was truly free at last.

She put a hand on her hip. She was still slender, but she had developed healthy curves. 'I think I'll leave being Storm Clements to you. You're a lot better at it than I was.'

'Actually, I don't really like any of the names you've had in the past.' He reached a hand and touched her hair. It was as soft as it looked.

'Why not?' Confusion flashed through her eyes.

He chuckled. 'Because I reckon you've tried every combination there is with your name apart from the best one. Tori Clements. I kind of like that. It has a nice ring to it.'

She smiled slowly as his words registered. Her look became playful again. 'So what are you going to do about it?'

He shrugged, amused. 'Ask Prince and Rachel to adopt you?'

'No way! That would make you my uncle!'

He pretended to be offended. 'And what's so wrong with having me as your uncle? I happen to be a very good uncle.'

She lifted her chin. 'It would be wrong to kiss you if you were my uncle.'

Her boldness surprised him. But wasn't this what he had been wanting? A true indication of her feelings? She was finally letting herself love and be loved. He matched her teasing look. 'Why? I kiss my niece.'

Then he lowered his face until their noses almost touched and his eyes were looking directly into hers. 'Not like this, though.' Gently, he met her lips with his own. He kissed her softly at first, and then with more intensity.

She drew in a deep breath, then murmured against his lips. 'I've been dreaming about this.'

'Hmm? What else have you been dreaming about?'

She bit her lip, looking self-conscious. 'Just you. Being with you for always.'

He smiled down at her. He never thought he'd feel this way about anyone; never thought he'd *let* himself feel this way. But he hadn't known what he was missing out on.

Her eyes were searching his. 'What's going on with us?'

He grinned. 'I think it's called love. Soppy, emotional, risky love. And something so much deeper too.'

'Something that will last?'

'Well, I think we're a bit young to be committing to marriage yet, but I sure hope so. For now, let's just wait and see what amazing things God has planned for our future, hey?'

She lifted her arms around his neck and he kissed her again before lifting his eyes to heaven.

Thank you God, for teaching us to trust you. And each other.

He knew it was trust in God and their obedience that led them back to the circus and into each other's arms. The storm was over and a rainbow of promise filled the sky.

Also by Jenny Glazebrook

Blaze in the Storm
Bonnie's world is happy and carefree until Blaze Clements and his horse-crazy family arrive from the circus. Is believing in God the only way to make sense of the tragedy that strikes?

Heart of Thunder
Beauty Clements hates her name – along with everything and everyone. What will it take to get through to her? Can God's love and forgiveness free her from her past?

Clouds of Prayer
Prince Clements captured Rachel's heart the moment he left the circus and rode into her school. But she is a minister's daughter and Prince has no time for God.

Mist of the Morning
Roy can't work out if clumsy Misty Clements is clever and manipulative or if she is just as lost in the world as she seems. What is she hiding from him?

Forgiving Sky
Sky Clements refuses to accept anything from the father who abandoned her as a baby. It will take a miracle to forgive him. But what if that miracle is just waiting to happen?

www.ingramcontent.com/pod-product-compliance
Lightning Source LLC
Chambersburg PA
CBHW031245120726
47905CB00002B/720